The Divas:
Diamond

CH

The Divas:
Diamond

Victoria Christopher Murray

Pocket Books
New York London Toronto Sydney

POCKET BOOKS
A Division of Simon & Schuster, Inc.
1230 Avenue of the Americas
New York, NY 10020

First Pocket Books trade paperback edition March 2008

POCKET and colophon are registered trademarks of Simon & Schuster, Inc.

For information regarding special discounts for bulk purchases, please contact Simon & Schuster Special Sales at 1-800-456-6798 or business@simonandschuster.com.

Manufactured in the United States of America

10 9 8 7 6 5 4 3 2 1

Library of Congress Cataloging-in-Publication Data

Murray, Victoria Christopher.
   Diamond / Victoria Christopher Murray.—1st Pocket Books trade pbk. ed.
       p. cm.—(Divas)
   Summary: In Los Angeles, California, four fifteen-year-old best friends, Diamond, Aaliya, Veronique, and India, form a gospel singing group in order to compete in a talent contest that could take them all the way to New York City and a quarter of a million dollar prize.
   ISBN-13: 978-1-4165-6216-0
   ISBN-10:   1-4165-6216-8
  [1. Singers—Fiction. 2. Gospel music—Fiction. 3. Best friends—Fiction. 4. Friendship—Fiction. 5. Contests—Fiction. 6. African Americans—Fiction. 7. Family life—California—Fiction. 8. Los Angeles (Calif.)—Fiction.] I. Title.
   PZ7.M9663Dic 2008
   [Fic]—dc22

                                                2007040185

Acknowledgments

First and foremost, I always thank my Lord and Savior, Jesus Christ. People often ask me where I get the ideas, the stories, the titles—it all comes from God. I feel so blessed that He uses my fingers to deliver these messages through books. There is nothing better than living my life and using my gifts for Him.

I am so excited to be doing this teen series. I want to provide stories that are totally entertaining but center on God. And I am blessed to have a professional team that understands my objective. Thank you, Brigitte Smith, and everyone at Pocket Books for giving me this opportunity. We're just beginning, but I am already enjoying this ride. To my agent, Elaine Koster, who believed in this idea and supported me from the very beginning. And to Stephanie Lehmann, who not only took my proposal and ran with it, but taught me how to really get inside the mind of, and use the voice of, a teenager. I learned so much from you. This idea began in my head, and it was Jacquelin Thomas who helped me think it all through and Kimberla Lawson Roby who encouraged me to do it. I am honored to call both of you friends!

To all the readers who have supported me over the years and asked if I was ever going to do something for teens—here it is. I pray that young girls and those who are young at heart all have the opportunity to enjoy Diamond's story.

$\mathcal{W}$e're gonna be so paid!"

I waved my magazine in the air and dumped my messenger bag onto the lunch table. I waited for my crew to say something, but not one of them even looked at me.

"Hello? Anybody home?"

India stuffed half a hot dog into her mouth. "I heard you."

"So, if you heard me, why aren't you excited?" But I wasn't just talking to India. I wondered what was wrong with Veronique and Aaliyah, too.

"Because," Aaliyah began, not taking her eyes away from whatever book she was reading, "you're *always* excited about something, Diamond."

"And what's wrong with that?" I asked. "I'm fifteen and fine! I'm supposed to be excited."

Veronique unplugged one of the earplugs from the MP3 player we'd given her for her birthday. "You are so the drama queen."

"Whatever, whatever. Call me what you want; I'm going to be a paid drama queen. And, I'm gonna let y'all ride because I love you and I'm special like that."

Veronique tried not to grin, but I knew she was feelin'

me. She pushed her earplug in place and lay back on the bench.

When no one said anything else, I said, "Don't you want to know how I'm gonna make you rich?"

"Diamond," India said, now chomping on French fries, "you're already rich."

"Nuh-huh. My parents have money, but they've told me and my brother over and over that it's their money, not ours." I shrugged. "But it doesn't matter 'cause in less than a year, the cash will be flowin' my way."

Veronique sat up. "Okay, I'll bite. What's up?"

One down. But I still had to stare at India like she'd stolen something before she paid me more attention than she did her French fries. And then, we all had to give Aaliyah the evil eye before she—with a sigh—half-closed her book.

With their eyes on me now, I snapped the magazine open to the centerfold. "Peep this!"

India, Veronique, and Aaliyah stared at the pages that announced the gospel talent search, but then just as quickly, India tossed a handful of French fries into her mouth, Veronique stuffed her ears with the plugs again, and Aaliyah went back to her book as if she'd never stopped reading.

I could not believe them. I loved my crew like they were my own sisters. In fact, we always said we were sisters, since none of us had any biological sisters. But today I wanted to give them all back to their mothers.

"What are you guys doing?" I waited a moment. When no one answered me, I bounced on top of the bench even though I had rolled up my skirt so that it would look like a mini. "Hello!" I yelled. "Does anyone besides me want to be a star?"

There were plenty of cackles from everyone else in the school yard, but nothing from my crew.

Finally, Veronique said, "You're the one who wants to be a star, my sistah."

"Well, yeah," I said, wondering why she was taking the time to state the obvious. "Because I was born to be one. And we live in L.A. We're supposed to be stars."

"I don't want to be one." India wrinkled her nose like she smelled something nasty.

"Me neither," Veronique and Aaliyah piped in.

"That's un-American," I said. "But this is about more than just being a star." I paused, letting the drama build. "What if I told you we were about to be paid a million dollars?"

That made Veronique take both plugs from her ears. "A million dollars? Tell me more, my sistah."

"Actually, it's more like two hundred and fifty thousand."

Aaliyah lifted her eyes from her book just long enough to say, "That's a long way from a million."

I rolled my eyes. Leave it to the analytical one to take my words literally. Still, I said, "Not by much. And anyway, that's just the start. When we win this contest, we'll get phat contracts and we'll certainly have a million dollars then. Probably more."

"Go for it," Aaliyah said.

I rolled my eyes toward heaven and asked the Lord to help me. "You're supposed to be the smart one. Didn't you read that this is a group competition?"

"So, that's what this is about," India said. "You need a group; you need us." She shook her head. "And I thought you were telling us about this because you loved us."

"Love you, I do. But on the real, I need you." I paused, lifted the magazine, and began reading, "Glory 2 God Productions is the latest record label to take advantage of the *American Idol* phenomenon. Announcing their own talent show, G2G president Roberto Hamilton said, 'We're looking for fresh talent with hip-hop flavor, but with the heart and love for the Lord. We're excited about the possibilities. Our plan is to make the winning group superstars.'" I slammed the magazine shut. "They are obviously talking about us."

"We're not a group," Veronique said.

Inside, I moaned. "Not yet. But if you guys would pay attention and start dreaming this dream with me, we'd have a group in"—I looked at my watch—"how long will it take for us to come up with a name?" When no one answered, I whined, "Come on."

Veronique nodded her head slowly, as if she'd had a little peek into my dream. I knew I could count on her. Even though I considered India and Aaliyah my best friends, too, I was closest to Vee, which was what we called her. Veronique was quite different from me; she was different from all of us. With her wild, bronze-colored fro, the little gold stud in her nose, and wooden and beaded bangles up and down her arm, she looked like she was some kind of flower child from the sixties. I think she got her style from her mom. It was kind of old-fashioned to me, but I loved Veronique anyway. And I loved her even more right about now.

I clapped my hands. "So, you're in?"

Veronique said, "I didn't say that. I need to know more."

I sighed as India and Aaliyah looked at me like they

agreed with Veronique. What more did they possibly need? Sometimes I wondered how we all became friends, because I was so far ahead of them it wasn't even funny. I believed in dreams that they hadn't even begun to imagine. But I stayed with them because India, Veronique, and Aaliyah needed me. India needed me to help her with her self-confidence, Veronique needed me to show her life's possibilities, and Aaliyah needed me . . . well, I wasn't sure what Aaliyah needed from me because she always acted like she didn't need anybody. But I loved them all.

I said, "Okay, what else do you need to know besides the fact that Glory 2 God Productions is doing a national talent search to discover us?"

"Are we old enough to enter?" India asked as she dumped her empty food containers into the trash.

"This is a teen competition, so you have to be between the ages of thirteen and eighteen. I guess nineteen is too close to twenty. And after that, all we need is to be sponsored by our church."

"Sponsored? What does that mean?" Aaliyah asked.

"I don't know, but whatever it is, Pastor Ford will do it for us."

"Are you sure?" Veronique asked. "Pastor's never heard us sing."

"What are you talking about? We sing in church every month."

Aaliyah said, "You want to enter the entire choir in this contest?"

I looked at Aaliyah wide-eyed. There was no doubt she was the brains; Aaliyah had never received anything less than an A since elementary school. But sometimes she acted like her brain went on vacation. "Of course I'm not talking about the entire choir. I'm talking about just us. If we can sing in the choir, why can't we form our own little group?" When they said nothing, I added, "Okay, let me break this down to you like you're two-year-olds: the four of us form a group, go to church, get sponsored, send in the applications, begin practicing, sing some songs, do some steps, win . . . and then get the big bucks."

"I like that big bucks part," Veronique said.

"So, you're in?" I asked.

India, Veronique, and Aaliyah looked at each other, and inside, I prayed, *Please, God, let my crew have some sense.*

Slowly, India and Veronique nodded. But Aaliyah held out her hand. I tossed her the magazine, then watched her look over the article.

"This says that the participants are responsible for their own expenses. . . ."

"Expenses?" Veronique frowned.

Aaliyah continued, "All travel, lodging, and any expenses associated with the contest will be the responsibility of the applicants."

"So, hold up." Veronique stopped Aaliyah. "How much money are they talking about?"

"According to this," Aaliyah paused and read some more, "if we win in Los Angeles, we'd have to pay our way to San Francisco. Then to . . ."

Veronique shook her head. "I can't afford to be in this contest."

I was about to burst with frustration. "Why're you worrying about the money right now? Let's just form the group. If we're serious, you know my parents will cover everything."

"No way," Veronique said, lying back down on the

bench. "My mother is not about to spend money she doesn't have. At least that's what she's always telling me."

"I said don't worry about the money."

"We have to think about how much this will cost. If we win this, like you say, we'd have to go all the way to . . . ," Aaliyah said as she looked down at the magazine, "New York and Miami."

Veronique bolted up from the bench. "New York? When would we go to New York?"

I guess somehow money wasn't a problem for her now.

"That's where the semifinals are going to be," Aaliyah said.

"I always wanted to go to New York." Veronique bit her lip, then said to India and Aaliyah, "Maybe we should talk to Pastor Ford and see what she thinks."

"Okay, I'm willing to start there." I was doing everything I could to hold in my excitement. "So, are y'all ready to roll with me?" I held out my hand, and after a couple of moments, Veronique gave me a high five. Then, India. And although I could tell she wasn't really feeling this, Aaliyah finally did the same.

"You know singing ain't my thing," Aaliyah pouted. "But y'all my sisters, so when you roll, I roll."

I grinned. None of them were as excited as I was, but all they needed was a little time. India, Veronique, and Aaliyah had no idea how blessed they were to have me. I was on my way to making us all stars!

2

God was on my side!

I was sure of it as I held back the drapes and peeked through the living room window. My dad eased his Navigator into the driveway. If I'd been just a kid, I would've run right outside to meet him. But since I was much too mature to do that, I just waited and planned my next move. I walked back and forth in the living room as if I was calm, but my cool didn't last and I rushed to the door.

"Hi, Daddy," I greeted him before he could even get inside. I wrapped my arms around his neck and kissed his cheek.

"Whoa, cupcake. Let me get in," he said.

But I could tell by the way he grinned that he was loving it! Loving every bit of the attention that I gave him.

I was the walking definition of a daddy's girl. It wasn't hard for me—I looked exactly like my father. We shared the same brown eyes framed under bushy brows. My chestnut complexion matched his to a T. And when my dad had hair, it had been as black and as thick as mine. But our best feature was our dimples—both of us just had one in our left cheek.

My dad stepped into the foyer. It took a lot for me to

just stand there, but I waited by the front door as he dropped his briefcase next to the divan, then scanned through the mail sitting on top of the glass table.

I waited and waited. And then I couldn't wait any more. "How was your day, Daddy?"

He looked at me, tossed the mail back on the table, and with a tiny grin said, "How much is this going to cost me?"

I opened my eyes wide. "What?"

He loosened his tie, and when he walked into the living room, I followed right behind him. He asked, "Are you going to tell me how much you need?" before he flopped onto the sofa.

I grinned. "I don't want any money. At least not yet." I grabbed the magazine from the table, then bent down in front of him and flipped through the pages.

My father pulled his glasses from his pocket. "So, which one of your magazine schemes do you want me to look at today?"

"This is no ordinary magazine, Daddy. This is *Gospel NOW* and they've got this ridiculous contest."

"Ridiculous? Is that good?"

I laughed. "Definitely. India, Veronique, Aaliyah, and I want to form a gospel group so that we can compete. It's kinda like *American Idol*, but with a gospel flavor. They're looking for fresh talent, and I know we can win."

He read and I talked, explaining all the details, which I already knew by heart. "Daddy, what I love is that we'll be able to combine our love for singing with our love for the Lord."

He stopped reading and looked at me over the top of his glasses. "Love for singing with love for the Lord? You're laying it on a bit thick, don't you think?"

Okay, he got me. I guess my dad knew a con when he heard one. He should; Linden Winters was a politician, a city councilman. Veronique said most politicians were cons or crooks. Not that my dad was either one, but I guess he'd worked with enough of them to recognize game.

"Daddy, I really want to do this," I whined. "Please, Daddy."

I held my breath as he took another look at the magazine. "I'm going to need to check this out, but it sounds interesting."

He was getting close to saying what I wanted to hear. "Yeah, this might be fun for you."

"Thank you," I sang and grabbed his neck, hugging him as tight as I could.

"Now wait a minute," Daddy said, pulling away. "It sounds good to me, but we still have to run this past your mother."

I groaned; why did he have to bring her into this? Not that I didn't love my mother. Elizabeth Winters was fierce. My mother was an appellate court judge in the Los Angeles superior court system. She'd been a judge since I was in kindergarten, overseeing all kinds of cases. The judge was no joke; my mother was the real deal.

Problem was, she acted like a judge all . . . the . . . time. Sometimes when she talked to me I felt like she was sitting on the bench ready to bring down the gavel right on top of my head. It wasn't going to be easy convincing the judge. But if there was one person who could get my mom to take off her judge's robe, it was my dad.

He glanced at the grandfather clock. "Your mother should be home soon." He stood. "Did Carmen leave?"

"Uh-huh. She said dinner's in the oven."

"Okay." Daddy stood. "We'll talk to your mother when she gets home," he said before he walked up the stairs.

I stood at the bottom, watching until my dad was out of sight. Then I clapped my hands. My dad was in my pocket. All I had to do now was soften up the judge. But how could I do that?

Then I got an idea, and I rushed into the kitchen.

"Hi, Mother." I kissed the judge on her cheek, then waved to Jimmy, her driver, who took her to and from the court-house every day.

My mother kissed me back, then did exactly what my father had done thirty minutes before—she stood in the foyer and scanned through the mail. "Something smells good; is Carmen still here?"

"Nope," I said, taking my mother's briefcase from her hand. "Carmen left right after I got home. I just set the oven to keep everything warm." I paused. "And I set the table, too."

Now my mother looked at me. Her eyebrows were raised so high they were almost at the top of her forehead. "What's up with you?"

I don't know why my parents always thought there was something behind my good deeds. Shoot, sometimes I could do nice things just because.

I shrugged. "Nothing. I just wanted to set the table so you wouldn't have to do it after such a long day at work."

My mother squinted like she was trying to see me better. "Oh, now I know for sure that you're up to something, Diamond Winters."

"Yes, she is." We both turned to see my father strutting

down the stairs with his favorite pipe dangling from his hand. He kissed my mother and then, with his arms still around her, he said to me, "Let your mother get comfortable before we talk."

"What's this about?" my mother asked, looking back and forth at my father and me.

"We'll talk," he said. "You go on upstairs and relax."

But I didn't see why I should have to wait when my mother was standing right here, right now. Just like before, I couldn't wait. "Mother, we want to form a gospel singing group for this contest. Can we, please? Please?"

"Whoa," she said, stepping back a bit. "What contest? What group?"

Shaking his head, my father strolled into the living room. "I guess we're going to have this discussion now whether I want to or not." He filled his pipe with tobacco and glared at me. But I could tell he wasn't mad. The way the ends of his lips twitched like he was going to laugh at any moment gave him away.

"So," my mother started, "tell me what's going on."

My parents sat side by side on the sofa as I made my case. I told them how I'd found out about the contest, and how my crew all agreed to do it. I left out the part about no one being as excited as I was, because as soon as we got started, I knew India, Veronique, and Aaliyah would be right with me. I ended with, "Of course, we won't do anything until we check with Pastor Ford. But I know she'll agree with us because Glory 2 God is such a good company." I stopped, out of breath, then thought about the one thing that I knew would get them. "And the good thing is that this will keep the four of us focused on God."

There was a moment of silence and then . . . they

laughed! I couldn't believe my mother and father were sitting there laughing at me.

"I'm serious," I said.

It seemed as if five minutes passed before my mother held up her hand. "I know you're serious, dear," she said, still chuckling like my words were the best joke she'd heard in a long time. She turned to my father. "Well, this is quite a project. What do you think?"

My father puffed on his pipe. "I think this could be good. I want to check out everything, of course. . . ." I smiled as he paused. "And we'll talk to Pastor Ford and the other parents. . . ."

I clapped my hands.

"But first . . ."

Oh, no. Here comes the judge. Whenever my mother was ready to shoot down one of my ideas, she started with "But first . . ."

Mother continued, ". . . we need to take a look at your calendar."

I groaned. My mother seemed to forget that I was just fifteen. I didn't have a calendar.

"I don't want this to get in the way of your studies," the judge said.

"It won't. I promise."

My mother gave me one of those looks—one of those mother-eye looks that meant she didn't believe a word I said. "Maybe you should give up the dance team."

"Mother, why?" Since I was fifteen—a mature fifteen—I didn't want to whine. But the judge made that hard. "I can do both. We'll probably only have to rehearse once or twice a week for the group. And the dance team practices are only twice a week."

"That sounds like a lot to me."

"But I haven't even made the squad yet. You're taking me off the team before I even try out."

There was that mother-eye again.

"Mother, I promise, I can handle everything." Then I turned to my ace in the hole. "Daddy, please? I know I can do it. I can do the dance team and this group."

My mother said, "And school?" as if I'd forgotten the most important thing.

"Definitely school." I tried to put enough confidence in my voice to convince them. "I'll keep my grades up." I added, "And my grades might get even better because I'll be spending more time with Aaliyah. She'll make all of us study."

"Well . . ." The judge sounded like she still wasn't sure.

But then my dad piped in, "I think you can handle it."

Another moment, and then, "Okay," my mother agreed.

I squealed and jumped on both of them, kissing my father, then hugging my mother. "I promise I'm going to make you proud."

"We're already proud of you, dear," my mother said, rising from the sofa. "Now, I want to get out of these clothes."

"Okay." I dashed toward the staircase. Taking the steps two at a time, I yelled over my shoulder, "I've got to call my crew and let them know."

"Just be down for dinner in ten," I heard my mother say just before I closed my bedroom door.

I was so excited that I was trembling. This was the best thing that had ever happened to me. All my life I wanted to be a star, and now it was finally happening.

I grabbed my hairbrush, then jumped on top of my

bed. I pretended that everything in my room—my dresser, my desk, my computer, my TV, my bookshelves, and all of my family pictures—was my audience. And I was about to give them the performance of my life.

"We flyin' first class up in the sky," I sang into my brush like it was a microphone. *"Poppin' champagne, livin' my life."* I jumped around on my bed, waved my hands in the air. *"The glamorous, the glamorous life!"*

The glamorous life—that would be me! Me and my girls.

My girls! I'd almost forgotten about them. I needed to check in, see what kind of progress they'd made with their parents.

First I called India, then Veronique and Aaliyah. "It's on," I told them. All of their parents had agreed to at least a meeting, too. Only India was as excited as I was, but I wasn't worried about Veronique and Aaliyah. I knew that once we got together with Pastor Ford, everyone would begin to see what I saw—the glamorous life.

"Diamond," my mother called through the intercom.

I jumped up and pressed the Talk button. "I'm coming." But I rushed back to my bed. I had one more call to make. I had to leave a message for Pastor Ford.

3

I was so pumped up that I had to step out of the room for a moment. Everyone was in there waiting for Pastor. I was surprised when my dad stayed for this meeting after church—usually he left these kinds of things to the judge. But his being there let me know how much he believed in me.

India was there with her mom, Ms. Tova. And I was really glad to see Veronique mom, Ms. Lena, because Veronique hadn't been sure her mother would be able to take time away from he ekend job. Even Aaliyah's dad, who was the deputy c f police, had made time for this. It was clear that th nts got it—they were feelin' me.

"Diamond?"

I was so busy thinking that I h n't even noticed Pastor Ford come up to me

"Are you okay?" she asked.

"I'm fine. I was just waiting for you."

Pastor put her arm around me. "Seems like you've come up with quite the idea, young lady."

I grinned and followed her inside the conference room. All talking stopped. I stood to the side as our parents hugged Pastor Ford, and then they all chatted like they were friends. That's what I liked about our pastor; she might have been old—I think she was fifty or something—but she was down. She was just like us.

"Let's get started." Pastor Ford motioned for us to stand and hold hands.

I bowed my head, but I didn't pay too much attention to Pastor's prayer. All I wanted to do was shout *Hallelujah* and get to planning. We had a lot of work to do if we were going to be stars.

I couldn't believe how fast this was moving. A week ago, all I had to look forward to was trying out for the varsity dance team. But now I was on my way to one day being featured on *Cribs* or having my own *Style Star* episode. Or even better, I could be on MTV. I could see it now—*The Fabulous Life of Diamond Winters!* Or maybe they would change it—just for me—to *The Glamorous Life of Diamond Winters!*

When Pastor said, "Amen," I was the first one to raise my head.

"Well," Pastor Ford began, "I was just telling Diamond that I think she's come up with quite an idea." She glanced at her notes. "I spoke to the president of Glory 2 God Productions—Roberto Hamilton—and it seems as if they want a group out there that can rival all of this mainstream stuff. So, this contest is legit. Roberto is very excited about having Hope Chapel as one of the entries. They're not accepting everyone—only about twenty groups—all sponsored by their church." She paused and looked at me and my crew. "I think you girls will represent us well."

"Pastor, I have a question."

I groaned when my mother raised her hand, but then

when they all looked at me, I realized I'd made that sound out loud.

I coughed, trying to play it off. But that didn't stop my protest inside. Why did the judge have to ask questions? Hadn't she heard the pastor? If Pastor Ford said it was okay, it was okay. All my mother needed to think about was when she should write the check.

"Who's going to work with the girls?" my mother asked.

"I've asked Sybil Scott," Pastor Ford said in response to my mother's question. "She couldn't be here tonight, but she's as excited about this as I am."

Then India's mother really tried to upset me with her question. "My only concern," Ms. Tova said, "is their schoolwork. How are they going to be able to do this and keep up in school?"

Usually Ms. Tova—who I sometimes called Drama Mama—was my favorite. Not only was she gorgeous but as a former top model, she was still fierce with her fashion. And from one fashionista to another, she recognized that I had special flava. Every time I went to India's house, Ms. Tova would give me her European magazines: *Elle*, *Style*, and then, my favorite—*This City Paris France* magazine. That was a long name, but it was a must-have for a girl like me.

"You know I'm not going to let anything interfere with school," Pastor Ford said to Ms. Tova. "I can't imagine that they would need to meet more than once, maybe twice a week. But schedules will be passed by all of you first."

Now that the parents knew that they had complete control, I hoped that would be the last question. Then Aaliyah's father raised his hand, and it was like a flood came into the room. The grown-ups just wouldn't stop.

With each question, I slid further down in my seat. They were talking about things that had nothing to do with the contest. Questions about schoolwork and who would travel with us and how many hours of practice. Not a bit of this would matter once we were stars.

Finally, there was silence. Until Pastor Ford said, "Lena, you've been so quiet. Do you have any questions?"

"Well," Ms. Lena began, "this all sounds good, but I'm afraid Vee won't be able to be part of it."

"What?" I exclaimed and then closed my mouth when everyone in the room over thirty—and Aaliyah—gave me the mother-eye.

Ms. Lena continued, "I know this could be a good experience, but it's clear that it's going to cost some money, and I'm not in the position right now for Vee to do this."

I could not believe what I was hearing. With the way Veronique slipped down in her seat as if she were trying to get under the table, I knew she couldn't believe her mother either. Veronique always hated when her mother talked in public about how poor they were. I didn't think she was really poor. I mean, they lived in a nice apartment and everything. Ms. Lena did have to work two jobs to take care of Veronique and her four brothers, but none of that should have even mattered. Veronique was my girl, and if I was in the group, then she was in the group. Trust. Because that's just the way I lived.

Plus, we needed her. I mean, my voice was decent, and so was India's. But Veronique and Aaliyah . . . the two of them could blow! With them, we couldn't do anything but win.

Pastor Ford said, "I did ask Mr. Hamilton about expenses. He explained that we would be responsible for all costs. I haven't had time to work out a budget and think about how we would handle this—"

"Don't worry about any of this, Pastor."

I grinned. I knew the judge would come through.

My mother continued, "You come up with the budget for the girls and Linden and I will cover it." My father nodded his approval. My parents were da-diggity bomb!

Ms. Tova said, "Thanks, Elizabeth, but I got this for India."

Then Mr. Heber, Aaliyah's father, added that he had his daughter covered, too.

"All right, then," my mother said to Ms. Lena. "We'll take care of Diamond and Veronique." She looked at Veronique. "You know we love her as if she was a Winters."

"But she's not a Winters," Ms. Lena said with an attitude. "She's a Garrett. And the Garretts don't have the money to do this."

"No problem," my mother said, totally clueless to the angry glance Ms. Lena gave her. "Veronique needs to be in the group. She has the voice of an angel. And who knows?" my mother said as she pulled out her checkbook. "This might be the girls' big break. Soon Veronique could be buying you a house."

The look Ms. Lena gave my mother stopped everyone in the room—everyone except for my mother, who flipped through her wallet looking for a blank check.

My father said, "Elizabeth, put your checkbook away."

My mother frowned but did as she was told.

Then Pastor Ford said, "I'd like to speak to the Winters and the Garretts alone."

It seemed like India's mother and Aaliyah's father couldn't move fast enough. India and her mother were the first ones to rush to the door. "We'll be in the sanctuary," Ms. Tova said. And then Aaliyah and her father followed.

Veronique scooted her chair closer to mine. And under the table, she held my hand.

When we were alone, Pastor Ford said, "Lena, you seem upset."

I wondered what was Pastor's first clue. Had it been the way Ms. Lena glared at my mother? Or was it the way her arms were folded? Or maybe just the way her leg shook under the table, making her chair rock.

"I am upset, Pastor," Ms. Lena said. "Because I said I cannot afford this and I don't appreciate being embarrassed this way."

"Lena, I am so sorry," my mother said. "I didn't mean to offend you. I just didn't want you to be concerned about the money."

"I'm always concerned about money," Ms. Lena said. "That's my life. I'm sorry if you don't like it."

Pastor Ford lifted her hand. "Lena, you know Elizabeth didn't mean anything. She made the offer straight from her heart."

"That's true, Lena." It wasn't often I heard my mother speak in that gentle tone. "I'm really sorry if I offended you."

It took a moment for Ms. Lena to unfold her arms and grant my mother a half smile.

Pastor Ford said, "Okay, so what I want to do is to figure out how all of the girls will do this. This is great, not only for them but for our church. We'll figure out a way to make this happen. Agreed?"

It was hard to say no to Pastor Ford. Especially since she was standing as if it had already been decided.

When Pastor Ford went into the hallway to get India and Aaliyah and their parents, my mother rushed to Ms. Lena.

"I'm sorry," she whispered again.

Ms. Lena took her hand. "I know you are. And forgive me, too." She shook her head. "It's just that I don't want to be a burden on anyone."

"You're not," my mother said. "But I understand what you were saying."

They were still hugging when the others came back into the room.

"Okay," Pastor Ford said. "Let's take a look at this calendar and start planning."

I took out my notepad. Finally, we were getting to what was important.

"Sybil wants to meet with the girls this week," Pastor Ford said. "What about Tuesday evening?"

I was just too excited. Tuesday was just fine with me. In fact, Tuesday just wouldn't get here fast enough.

4

I dropped my bag, then slid to the floor. Veronique stepped over me and peeked inside the gym.

"Don't you want to peep the competition?" she whispered.

"What competition?"

She laughed. "See, that's why you're my sistah." After a pause, she asked, "You nervous?"

I pulled one of my favorite magazines from my bag and flipped back to the article I'd been reading: "What Do Boys Think?" "Nope, not nervous at all."

"Dang. I came to give you support, but you don't need me."

I grinned. "I'll always need you. But, as far as these try-outs"—I flicked my hand in the air—"I got this."

"I guess you do."

"With the way my life is going, of course I'm gonna make the dance team. Besides, I practiced all summer. And," I paused, "I'm not braggin' or nothin', but I'm good."

Veronique grinned. "Okay, but remember they only have two spots for sophomores."

"Whatever, whatever. One of those spots is mine. Shoot,

those girls would be crazy not to put me on the squad since we're on our way to becoming stars."

"You really think we got a shot with that contest? I mean, how many people do you think are entering?"

I slapped my magazine shut. "Well, in the city, only twenty churches. That's what Pastor said. And nationwide . . . I don't know and I don't care. Because we're the best, Vee. We're gonna win."

"That would be great. Especially if we get the chance to go to New York."

I didn't know why my girl was suddenly so interested in going to the Big Apple. "New York is overrated. I've been there so many times." I sighed, totally bored with the idea of being in the city. "One thing though, they do have great shopping."

"For that you need money."

I took a moment before I said, "I'm glad your mom's okay. It would have been ruined if she didn't let you be part of the group."

Veronique shrugged. "She's kinda excited about it, but she's still not gonna let your mom pay. Trust and know."

"I don't get it. If we have the money and my mom is willing to share it. . . ." I shook my head. I would never understand anyone over thirty.

Veronique said, "I get what my mom's saying. She's a proud Black woman who wants to take care of her own. That's what family pride is all about. So," Veronique took a breath, as if she wasn't sure whether or not she was ready to tell me something. "I'm going to help out; get a job and help my mom do this."

I laughed, but when Veronique didn't laugh with me, I

asked, "Vee, you're kidding, right?" She stayed quiet. I added, "We're fifteen; we're not supposed to work."

"Lots of kids work."

"Yeah, but lots of kids are not us. We have the contest, and we have school. What about the student council? Have you forgotten that you're the sophomore class president?"

"No, but I may have to give it up and run again next year."

"But you just got elected."

Veronique shrugged. "I had to make a choice. It's either the student council or our group. It's not like . . ."

Veronique kept talking, but I stopped listening. Jason Xavier, the star of our Holy Cross Prep basketball team, strutted past, bouncing a basketball. Behind him, a line of his boys followed, as if he was some kind of pied piper. He didn't look at me, but when a group of girls at the other end of the hall called his name, he leaned back, pointed his index finger at them, then disappeared into the gym.

I sighed and wondered what it would take for him to take one look at me.

Veronique asked, "Did you hear what I said?"

"Huh?"

"I said—"

Before my girl could continue, I whispered, "Isn't he fine?"

"Who?"

"Jason Xavier. Didn't you see him?"

"I wasn't looking."

"I could look at him all day."

Veronique shrugged. "He's all right."

"If he would just stop bouncing that ball and hanging

with his boys and just look at me. I tried to get his attention all last year."

"Well now, he's a senior."

"So what? Now I'm a sophomore. There's not that much of a difference."

"Okay, let's just say that he does notice you. And then he asks you out. Have you forgotten who you live with? Even if you were able to get past your father, the judge ain't havin' it. Trust and know."

"Whatever, whatever." But inside, I knew my girl was right. My mother had this stupid rule that I couldn't date until I was sixteen. And no matter how hard I worked my daddy, I couldn't get either one of them to budge. I didn't know why. All of the magazines said that being fifteen now was different than being fifteen back in the day. And I agreed. I mean, fifteen-year-olds today were much more mature. All my parents had to do was look at the things we had to deal with that they never had to.

But my daddy and the judge weren't hearing it. It was their rule, and as long as I lived in their house. . . . I sighed, just thinking about how many times I'd heard that tired old line.

I didn't know why I was thinking about all of this. Even if somehow, some way Jason noticed me, by the time I was sixteen, he'd be gone.

The gym door swung open, and Jayde Monroe, dressed in her green-and-gold squad uniform, marched out with a clipboard in her hand.

I bounced up from the floor. "Hey, Jayde."

"Diamond Winters?" She called my name as if she didn't know me.

"Yes," I said, standing in front of her face. I couldn't believe she was gonna play me like that. Jayde was the captain of the varsity dance team, but she was also the daughter of Grace Monroe, a councilwoman who worked with my father. Jayde and I had attended so many boring political events together and had spent so many hours complaining about wasting our time that we should have been BFFs. But here she was today, acting like a stuck-up senior, like she didn't know me, just because I was a sophomore. Fine! She could play her stupid game.

"Come with me," Jayde said as if she was somebody's boss.

Veronique gave me a "you got this" look before I grabbed my bag and followed Jayde into the gym.

"Okay," Jayde began, "which of our routines are you going to do?" She kept looking at her clipboard, as if she couldn't stand the thought of looking at me.

I told Jayde that I'd chosen the most difficult one. That got her attention. "No one has chosen that one all day. Okay, girl. Go for it." She stopped in front of the judge's table. "Do your thing. We'll call you when we're ready."

I dropped my bag, leaned against the wall, and stretched my legs. I did my best to keep my eyes away from the judges' table—not that I was intimidated, but there was no need to get worked up before I got on the floor.

"Okay, Diamond."

When I looked up it took everything within me to keep my mouth closed. Sitting at the end of the judges' table was Jason Xavier. And he was looking at me.

Five sets of eyes were on me as I strolled to the center of the gym, but there was only one pair that mattered. I looked straight at Jason, and when he licked his lips, I smiled. "Here we go," I said and jumped high into the air.

It was only a three-minute routine, but I had to do it four times. And now I felt as if I'd just cheered for an entire game. I stood in the middle of the floor as the five judges whispered and compared notes as if I wasn't there. Jason didn't even look at me.

"Okay." Jayde was the first one to speak. "Thanks, Diamond. We'll be in touch."

I waited a moment, hoping that Jason would say something. When he didn't, I muttered, "Thanks," then grabbed a towel from my bag before I slung the straps over my shoulder. I whipped around and was shocked to see Jason right behind me.

"Excuse me," I said, because I'd bumped into him. "I'm sorry." But I wasn't sorry. Not in the least—almost knocking him over gave me the chance to get up close and personal with the finest boy in the whole school.

"You were good out there," Jason said as he bounced his basketball. I wondered why he did that. Couldn't he leave it alone for one minute? "Really good," he added.

I tilted my head so that Jason could really see my dimple. "You think so? I'm not so sure," I said, even though I knew that I'd nailed it. There was no one at Holy Cross Prep who could dance better than me.

"Nah, nah. You were good."

"If you say so." I wondered if my smile was sexy—I hoped it was. That was one of the things the magazines said that boys loved—a sexy smile.

He stopped bouncing the ball and stepped closer. "I say so," he said. He pulled the towel from my hands, then dabbed at the perspiration that was on the edge of my forehead.

I was absolutely sure that I could go at any moment!

He handed me the towel, then backed away. "Just do me a favor and remember me when you make the team." He winked, pointed his index finger at me, then began bouncing the ball again. As if that was their sign, his boys rose from the bleachers and followed Jason out of the gym.

It took awhile for my legs to move and then I hurried into the hallway.

"You're not going to believe this." I grabbed Veronique the moment I spotted her. "Jason talked to me."

"So?"

"Did you hear me? Jason talked to *me*. But not only that, he was one of the judges. And he said that I was really good."

"I know you were good. I'm just not impressed with Jason."

"Why not?"

"Because he's so obvious."

"Obvious?"

"You know, cute in an obvious way. He's nothing special. You can find boys like him in any magazine."

"That's my point, Vee. He should be in a magazine. And one day, he will be. He'll be a star and I'll be one, too. We're a perfect match."

By the look in her eyes, I knew Veronique was about to call me crazy. But before she could open her mouth, Jayde came up behind us. She was with two other dance members who'd been at the judges' table. The way they smiled, I knew they were about to tell me that I had made the team.

Jayde said, "You were really good."

"Thanks."

Then her smile went away. "But if you want to make the team, remember that you're only a sophomore. Stay in your place."

I frowned, but before I could ask her why she was trippin', she and her friends strolled away as if they owned the school.

"What was that?" Veronique asked.

"She's just acting all stuck up because she's a senior, I guess. Whatever, whatever. I'm not gonna let her take my happy away. I don't have time to think about Jayde Monroe."

"You'd better think about her if you want to make the team."

"I got that. I'm on it, I know. But even if I didn't make it, it wouldn't be a big deal anymore."

"What? Being on the dance team is all you've been talking about."

"Yeah, but now, I got our group. And, Jason Xavier. Trust and know!" I mimicked her, then laughed at the way she folded her arms and frowned. But I didn't care what Veronique thought. Nothing was going to stop my flow. Right now, life just couldn't get any better than this.

5

I never did like the front pew.

The last time we sat in this row together, we had on little white robes and swimming caps and were about to be dunked under some water. I was so scared back then—I'd seen other people get baptized, but I was sure that I was going to be the first seven-year-old to drown in the baptismal pool.

But today I wasn't afraid of a thing. We were in the sanctuary waiting for Pastor Ford. So we all sat in the front pew—the row usually reserved for Christian big shots. And since that's what we were going to be, I sat down first and my crew followed me.

"I hope this won't take long," Aaliyah whined. "I have to get home; I have a trig test tomorrow."

I rolled my eyes. Aaliyah was my girl, but sometimes she just got on my nerves. Always talking about school. I couldn't tell if she was bragging about being in eleventh grade math while the rest of us were still struggling to get Bs in geometry or if she was complaining because she had to study. Knowing Aaliyah, she was bragging. She was the only teenager I knew who really loved to study.

"If I get home by nine," she continued, "I should be all right."

Enough already! But before I could shut her down, Pastor Ford and Sybil Scott strolled into the sanctuary.

"Hello, ladies," Pastor welcomed us.

After all the greetings, I could tell my crew was finally getting a little bit excited. India had been feeling me all along, and Veronique was in this just because she was my girl. But even Ms. You-Know-Singing-Ain't-My-Thang was grinning.

"I'm going to leave you ladies with Sybil, but I want you to know how proud I am. I know you're going to represent Hope Chapel well. We'll be supporting you. It's too bad this isn't one of those call-in shows, or I'd be making my hundred calls a week."

We all laughed.

"But we'll all be at the Kodak Theatre in November, and I'll be behind you in every way that you need. So now, I'll turn you over into the capable hands of Sybil."

I really liked Sybil and was glad that Pastor had chosen her. As the assistant minister of music, she'd worked with us in the youth choir. What was really cool was that she wasn't as old as anyone else Pastor could have assigned to us. And I'd seen her dance; sistah—like Veronique would say—could bust a move. We needed someone like her—hip and holy!

"I'm so excited to be working with you guys. And I have no doubt when we're finished in nine weeks, we'll be walking away with the city championship and on our way to the state finals."

"That's what I'm talking about," I said. The way my crew grinned, I knew they agreed with me.

"So," she continued, "there are a couple of things we have to decide—like what song to perform. Also, you'll be working with Turquoise; she's going to choreograph some moves for you ladies."

We all cheered to that news. Turquoise was just nineteen years old, but she had already starred on Broadway in *The Lion King*. Word was she turned down a gig in *The Color Purple* to attend USC. When I'd heard that, I thought she had lost her mind. No one better ever give me the chance to go to Broadway—one word like that, and I would be out of here.

"Before we pick a song, shouldn't we choose a name?" India asked.

"Definitely," I said. "We need something fierce."

"That's a good name," India said. "Fierce."

I scrunched my nose. And when Veronique and Aaliyah did as well, India slid back into the pew. Usually, I was the one to make her feel better, but I didn't have time for that right now.

"Our name should say something about who we are," Veronique said.

"That's a good idea," I agreed. "Maybe we should have the word sisters in the name."

"Not sisters, sistahs," Veronique said, putting emphasis on the way she said the word.

I sighed. "What's the difference?"

"Ebonics," Aaliyah piped in. "I'm not going to be part of any group that doesn't use proper English." After everyone moaned, Aaliyah added, "I would think our name is obvious."

Even Sybil had a look on her face as if she couldn't figure out the obvious thing Aaliyah was talking about. When no one said anything, Aaliyah sighed, like she was the only one who had any brains.

"Look at our names," she said.

If that was supposed to be a clue, she needed to give us another one.

"Okay, we have Diamond, India, Veronique and me, Aaliyah." Still nothing. Aaliyah raised her hands in the air as if she was pleading with God. "Look at the first letters of our names: D-I-V-A. Diva!" She paused, "And Sybil, you put the *S* in Divas."

It didn't even take a second for me to agree. "Yes! Because that's who we are. Divas."

Sybil laughed, then said, "Okay, that's a good start. But divas by itself won't work."

"What about something like Definitely Diva." I was so proud that I had made that alliteration. We'd just studied that in English, so I guess Mrs. Watson was right—some of this school stuff really did work in the real world.

"Okay," Sybil said.

But the way she said that, I knew she wasn't feeling it. And neither were my girls.

India raised her hand like she was in school. "What about Divine Divas?" she whispered, as if she was afraid to say it.

Divine Divas.

Sybil said, "I like that—what do you all think?"

"That'll work," Aaliyah said.

"I like it, too," I said, and then we all looked at Veronique to make sure that she agreed.

She shrugged. "It's all right. Would have been better if it had 'sistahs' or something in it."

"Whatever, whatever! You know this name is totally awesome."

Veronique grinned. "Yeah, it is. Okay, we're the Divine Divas."

The Divine Divas. The perfect name for a new group of stars.

6

It was so hard to concentrate.

My textbooks were spread all over my bed and my computer was in my lap, but none of that helped. I still couldn't focus on this paper that was due on Monday on Zora Neale Hurston. First I'd had to read a book that was written in like 1937, and now I had to write about her life. How could I think about someone who lived so long ago when my head was filled with the Divine Divas? I had such a good feeling about us. First of all, we were cute. We could dance. But best of all, we could sing. And Veronique and Aaliyah could do better than that—my girls could sang! I really believed—no, I knew—that we could win this thing.

But I had to find a way to get focused on my homework and keep my grades up, because my mother wouldn't waste one minute yanking my big break away from me if I didn't keep up in school.

I turned back to my computer, but then a second later, I jumped up when Fergie's voice vibrated through my Side-kick, *"We flyin' first class up in the sky. Poppin' champagne, livin' my life."* I glanced at the clock. It was just before ten, my phone cutoff time. And the judge was serious about that. I couldn't count the number of times she'd taken my cell away from me for violating *that* rule.

"Hello," I whispered.

"Diamond?"

I recognized her voice right away but decided that since she didn't know me, I didn't know her. "This is Diamond," I said, putting on the voice that I'd heard my mother use so often.

"This is Jayde Monroe from the dance squad."

"Oh, yes, Jayde," I said, continuing my façade. "How are you?" But inside, my heart pounded. I'd told Veronique that it didn't matter whether I made the team, but that wasn't true. The dance squad was the coolest part of the cheerleaders. I was already popular, but being part of the team would take me way up on the Who's Who radar. And I might be able to pick up a few steps for the Divine Divas.

"I'm calling with good news. You made the team."

I jumped off the bed and punched my fist through the air. But I made it seem like no big deal when all I said to Jayde was, "Thanks."

"You were really good," Jayde continued, "but not everyone was convinced that you were ready, because you're only a sophomore."

I wondered how many times she was going to throw that in my face.

She said, "I was the deciding vote that put you on the team."

"Thanks, Jayde. I'm ready."

"I think you are, but I also did it because our parents work together."

Oh, so now she wanted to remember that we did know each other.

"So, don't make me sorry," Jayde said. "And just stay in your place."

There it was again. What did "stay in your place" mean? It was probably some female drama. At least that's what the magazines called it. And even though we were at a Christian school, my mother always said that church folks had the most drama.

I really didn't care; it didn't matter to me what Jayde meant. Right now my world was too straight. So I just said, "I'll see you in practice on Wednesday," and hung up the phone right before I heard the knock on my door.

"Diamond?"

"Yes, Jud . . . I mean, yes, Mother."

The judge peeked inside my room. "I heard your phone ring. Just making sure you're off."

"I am," I said, holding my cell in the air for her to see. "It was Jayde Monroe. I made the team."

"That's terrific." My mother came into my bedroom and hugged me. "Just remember," and before she could continue, my smile went away, "you have a lot on your plate this year, but your grades are most important."

Inside, I groaned. But outside, I said, "Yes, Mother."

When she left me alone, I did my own little dance. Could my life get any better? Before I could answer my own question, Fergie sang out on my Sidekick again. I grabbed it fast and prayed that my parents hadn't heard that.

"Hello," I whispered.

"Hey, this is Jax."

Just his voice alone was going to make me stop breathing. "Hey, Jason," I said. "How did you get my number?"

"Call me what my peeps call me. Jax."

"Okay." I grinned and leaned back into my pillows. "But you didn't answer my question; how'd you get my number?"

"I get anything I want, if I really want it."

Now it was more than his voice that made me shiver.

"Hey, congrats on making the dance squad. I told you, you were good."

"Thanks, I'm excited. Now I'll be at all your games."

"True dat. Well, I gotta make this run, but holla at your boy."

And then he hung up. It was barely a minute. But then I stopped trippin' over how much time. Jax had called me! I scrolled to my incoming calls, but his number showed as Private. Oh well, I'd just ask him for his number the next time I saw him.

I wanted to get back to Zora, but there was no way I could concentrate on her now. Anyway, I had all weekend to do this report. Tonight, all I wanted to do was think about my glamorous life. The dance squad. The Divine Divas. And now, Jax. I was sure that he didn't call every girl. Especially not on a Friday night.

I just absolutely loved my life.

7

Can you believe Jax called me?" I asked my crew right before we stepped inside the church.

"You told us on Saturday, you told us on Sunday, you told us yesterday. You've told us a million times," Veronique whined.

I couldn't believe my girl was hatin' like this.

"Well, I think he's cute," India said.

"Thank you." I grinned and turned to Aaliyah.

"What?" When I didn't say anything more, Aaliyah said, "You don't wanna hear what I have to say."

"No, go on." Sybil had told us to meet her here in the rec room behind the sanctuary, and we still had ten minutes before she arrived. While we waited, all I wanted to do was talk about Jax.

"Okay," Aaliyah started, "I think he's just playing with you."

"Playing how?"

"He's a senior. What would he want with you?"

"Thanks a lot."

"You know what I mean. I'm just sayin' we're sophomores."

"You guys might just be sophomores. But I'm a fierce

sophomore. Why wouldn't Jax want me?" I snapped my fingers.

India laughed, but Aaliyah gave me one of those Aaliyah looks—with her eyebrows raised and her face all tight—like she knew more than me.

Aaliyah said, "Well, you're my girl, so I hope you're right. I hope he's not just messing with you."

Veronique said, "Me, too. Just be careful, my sistah."

I crossed my arms and poked out my lips. I couldn't believe what my crew was saying. I mean, the star of the basketball team, the most popular boy in school had called me and they weren't even impressed. What was wrong with them? It just made me mad the way they were hatin'!

I decided right then that I would never tell them anything else ever again. When Jax and I became boyfriend and girlfriend, they wouldn't hear it from me. Well, maybe I would tell India, because she wasn't acting like she was jealous. I would definitely share my good news with her.

Aaliyah said, "Okay, if we're finished talking about Jax, I think we should get started."

"How?" I asked, wanting her to hear my attitude. "Sybil's not here."

"We can at least talk about the songs so that when she gets here, we'll be ready."

All Aaliyah ever thought about was work. If she put that same effort into our friendship, maybe she would've had something nice to say about me and Jax. "What's the rush? We can wait."

"Look, I don't have time to sit around. Being part of the Divine Divas is going to be difficult enough with school. I'm just trying to be efficient."

Efficient? I hated when she talked like she was one of

our parents. "You know what, Aaliyah, I'm so tired of you. Maybe you're right. Maybe you don't need to be in this group. Maybe you should just quit."

All of their mouths were hanging wide open, but I didn't care. On the real, she'd worked my last nerve.

Aaliyah stared at me and then shrugged. "Nothing but a thang for me." She paused as if she wanted me to stop her.

All I said was, "Whatever, whatever."

"Okay, then, I'm out." She grabbed her bag and stomped toward the door.

India and Veronique stared me down, but I already felt bad. I hadn't believed that Aaliyah would really leave. I ran after her. "Wait, girl, I'm sorry."

Aaliyah folded her arms and stared like she wanted more.

I sighed. "I was just mad 'cause of what you said about me and Jax."

"There is no you and Jax," she said, giving me back attitude.

"I know. But I don't need you to tell me that."

"Well, if we don't tell you, who will?" Aaliyah tried to stay mad, but she was softening right in front of my face. "Okay," she said and hugged me. "It's just that I don't want to see you get hurt."

"I know."

"But if you like Jax, then I'll love him."

Just the sound of her voice told me that she wasn't really feeling what she was saying, but that was cool. I was just glad that she wanted to make peace.

Veronique said, "Remember, Diamond. We're sistahs. We have to tell each other the truth. All the time. Trust and know."

"She's right," India jumped in. "And just because we're honest doesn't mean that our feelings should be hurt."

The three of us looked at India like she had just landed from another planet. Talking about not getting feelings hurt—India's feelings were always hurt. She needed to take her own tip.

Veronique said, "So, we're sistahs all the way? No more dropping out?"

"Who's dropping out?"

None of us had noticed Sybil when she'd entered through the side entrance.

"No one," I said as we all strolled to where Sybil stood. She stared us down. "Uh-huh," she said. "Why don't you ladies have a seat?"

I could feel a lecture coming on.

"You know, maybe we should have talked about how difficult this is going to be," Sybil said. "I think you guys are seeing the glory, but this is gonna take guts. This is gonna take time. This is gonna take commitment. There are going to be days when you'll wonder why you ever started this. But I'm here for you. I'm in this all the way. So I don't want to hear anyone talking about dropping out. Is that clear?"

We nodded as if we'd been scolded.

"So do I have your commitment?"

"Yes," we said together. Then Sybil asked us to agree one at a time—as if she was trying to get a personal commitment from each of us.

"All right," she said. "Let's get to work. Tonight, I just want to work out the song. Now, the songs I suggested, I chose because all of them will showcase you ladies as a double threat. I want to show off your singing and your dancing. I want the crowd to hear your incredible voices, but at the same time, I want them dancing in the aisles with you. So, what do you think? Which song did you like?"

" 'I Don't Wanna Go to the Club,' " I said.

"That's the one I want," Aaliyah said.

"Me, too," India and Veronique added.

We were sisters again, all agreeing on the same song without ever discussing it. Too bad I couldn't get my crew to get with me and Jax the same way. But like Aaliyah always said, ain't nothin' but a thang. Once Jax and I were together, they would change their minds.

"Now," Sybil said, "the way I've arranged this song, each one of you will have a verse that you will sing solo."

Oh, this was too good!

Sybil continued, "But with this arrangement, we do need a lead."

Wow. I'd never thought about a lead singer. I just thought we'd all be singing together. Well, if everyone was honest, I should be the lead. I mean, the Divine Divas wouldn't even exist if it wasn't for me. I believed in our group more than my three girls combined.

But I wasn't sure if it was a good idea to nominate myself, so I sat on my hands and waited for one of my crew to do the right thing.

"Aaliyah should do the lead," India said.

"Definitely," Veronique agreed before I could say a word.

When they looked at me, I didn't have a choice. But before I could say yes, Aaliyah said, "No! I don't want it."

"Why not?" India asked. "You're the best singer."

"No, I'm not. Vee is. And I told you guys I'm only doing this because you asked. I don't really want to sing, and I'm not singing the lead. So, it's either Vee or one of you."

I was ready to jump in, but before I could, Veronique said, "Okay, I'll do it."

They all agreed; I didn't. But it didn't seem like it would be a good idea to start a fight over this.

As Sybil handed us the sheet music, I glanced at Aaliyah. Sometimes I couldn't figure her out. Why wouldn't she want to be front and center? Especially with her voice. Shoot, they would've had to ask me only one time and I would have taken that microphone and sung until my throat hurt.

Sybil pointed out the places where Veronique would be singing alone. I looked at all of her bars and had to force myself to get over it. I wouldn't be out front the way she was, but I was still going to be a star.

We stood around the keyboard and practiced a little, changing a few parts of Sybil's arrangement.

As we sang together, the picture of what was going to happen to us came into focus for me. Our lives were really going to change. One of the changes in my life was going to be Jason Xavier. Now that he had opened up the door, I was going to walk right in. I wasn't exactly sure how I was going to take that one phone call to the next level, but if there was anyone who could do that, it would be me. And anyway, once Jax heard about me and the Divine Divas, he would be begging me to be his girlfriend. I was sure of it. It was only a matter of time. Jason Xavier was going to be my man.

8

I had less than twenty-four hours before I had to turn in this paper on Zora Neale Hurston, so I needed every free moment today. I had already gotten an extension from Mrs. Watson. After a lot of begging, she'd given me ten days, but they had come with an automatic fifteen-point deduction—which meant that even if my paper was perfect, I wouldn't get more than a B.

I'd been cutting my schoolwork too close. It was harder than I thought. After only two weeks of dance team practices and Divine Divas rehearsals, I was already behind. Being a sophomore was different than being a freshman. All of these books I had to read and reports I had to write were making it tough.

I still had some free minutes before dance practice, so I leaned back on the bleachers. One more read through, and I would be ready to turn this paper in. Maybe I could get some points back if I turned this in today—nine days instead of ten days late.

"Hey, you."

I looked up and grinned. Jax stood over me, his basketball resting in the palm of his hand. "Hey, yourself."

"What you workin' on?" He leaned over, trying to get a peek at my paper.

"Nothing." I stuffed my report inside my bag. I didn't want him to walk away because he thought I was busy. I hadn't heard from him or seen him since he'd called me after I made the squad. I thought he'd forgotten about me already. "I was just reading. What are you doing here?"

"Looking for you."

"Really?"

But before Jax could say anything else, Jayde interrupted us. "Excuse me. Jax, can I speak to you"—she stopped and looked down at me—"privately?"

I almost told her to step back, but it wasn't like I wanted drama with the team captain. So I kept quiet.

"No prob," Jax said, then walked with her without saying a word to me.

I grabbed my paper from my bag, but even though I tried to read, I couldn't. Every few seconds I was peeking at Jax and Jayde standing at the edge of the gym. Jax leaned against the wall, bouncing his ball while Jayde talked. With the way she stood, her hands on her hips, I could tell she was more than just a little upset.

After a few minutes, Jax shook his head and walked out of the gym while Jayde stomped into the locker room.

Boy, I wanted to find out what that was all about, but then Tinesha, the co-captain of the dance team, came out of the locker room shouting and clapping her hands. "Okay, let's get started!"

She led us through our stretches before Jayde joined us. Through the whole two hours of practice, every time I looked at Jayde, I thought about Jax. What was their story? Was something going on between them? They didn't act like boyfriend and girlfriend. Jax didn't act like he had a girlfriend at all. I'd seen him around school with Jayde, but he was also with a lot of different girls, and it didn't seem like he was into any of them. Plus, if he was with Jayde, then why was he trying to talk to me?

At the end of practice, I was exhausted from more than just the dancing. It was the thoughts in my head that really made me tired. I grabbed a bottle of water from my bag, and when I turned around Jax was standing at the gym door, grinning.

I smiled.

He waved. Then he motioned for me to come over.

I checked over my shoulder, just to make sure that he was really talking to me. When I turned back and he pointed straight at me, I didn't waste any more time. But just as I was cutting across the floor, Jayde stepped up, blocking my way. If she hadn't been the captain, and if I hadn't been so focused on getting to Jax, I would have asked her what was her problem? But all I did was move around her as if she wasn't even there. I didn't want to hardly waste my time messing with Jayde when Jax was waiting for me.

"You looked good out there," Jax said.

"You were watching?"

"Yup." He stopped bouncing his ball for a moment. "And I liked what I saw."

Black girls don't blush—at least that's what I read in a magazine. But something was making my face hot. I needed to make Jax stop staring at me, so I asked, "Don't you have basketball practice?"

"Yeah, but I took a little time off so that I could see you." He leaned closer. "I got it like that 'cause I'm the star. But you know all about being a star, don't you?"

He was so close it was hard for me to breathe.

He said, "With a name like Diamond, you're already a star."

I tried to think of something absolutely brilliant to say, but I could hardly remember my own name.

Jax laughed and pulled a card from his jacket. He handed it to me, then, just like before, he walked away without saying a single word.

When he was gone, I glanced at the card. His name was printed, and right below were two words: *Call me.*

I turned the card over; it was blank on the other side. Call me? How was I supposed to do that without a telephone number?

But I was still impressed. Jax had his own business cards!

$\mathcal{W}$e're here," I shouted as India, Aaliyah, and I stepped into the church's bookstore.

"Ssshhh!" Veronique squealed, sounding like my mother. "You can't be making all that noise, my sistah. This is still church."

What was the big deal? It was Saturday; wasn't like a whole lot of folks, or even God, was hanging out here today. The church didn't look or feel anything like it would tomorrow. "Are you almost ready?"

"Yeah." Veronique put the books she was holding on the shelf.

"So how do you like this?" I looked around the bookstore. I couldn't believe that Veronique had actually gone through with her plan to work. At least it wasn't a real job where any of our friends would see her. This was church. She could always pretend that she was volunteering.

Even though this cut down on our hanging time, I was glad that Pastor Ford had come through for my girl. I didn't think the bookstore staff really needed someone to help them stack books, but that's how Pastor Ford was—she always had our back.

"It's all right," Veronique said. "I'm actually enjoying working here."

"This would be my dream." Aaliyah roamed through the aisles, looking like she was in a candy store. "I'd love to work around books."

What else is new? was what I wanted to say. But all I said was, "You like being around books because you like to study."

"No, sometimes I read for fun."

I said, "Read and fun? Can't use those words in the same sentence."

Aaliyah shook her head in that way that made me want to forget she was my sister. "That's 'cause you only like books with pictures."

I just knew Aaliyah wasn't dissin' me like that. "What're you tryin' to say?"

"I'm sayin' what I'm sayin'. You only like magazines. But you should try books sometimes. You don't know what you're missing."

"Whatever, whatever. Anyway, can we get out of here?" I jumped off the desk. "We've got a lot of shopping to do."

"I don't have any money," Veronique said.

I couldn't believe she was saying that. "You've been working for a week."

"First of all, I haven't been paid yet, and second, this money is not for me to spend. It's for the Divine Divas."

"Well, I'm talking about shopping for our group. We need to get to the mall and check out some outfits. We have to be fierce at the city finals."

"We've got weeks to plan," India said. "Let's not do that today."

India was the only girl I knew who didn't really like

shopping. Sometimes I thought it was because she was a little bit bigger and taller than the rest of us. But the way I saw it, you had to be proud of who you were. Anybody could rock any outfit, as long as they had confidence. I read a magazine article that said that sexy didn't have a dress size. On the real, that was a good tip.

"We need to start looking for the right outfit now," I told India. "We don't want to be forced to choose any old thing at the last minute and come up looking like an old church lady. I don't know 'bout y'all, but I've gotta look fly."

Aaliyah said, "Vee, are you ready? Or else we're going to be forced to listen to another one of Diamond's fashion lectures."

"Well, I am the fashionista." I laughed. But as soon as we stepped outside the store, all of my laughing stopped. This was the part I hated—where we had to wait for the bus. I wasn't a bus-riding kind of girl anymore.

The bus had never bothered me before, but now that I was fifteen and about to be a star, it didn't seem the right way for a girl like me to roll. I needed a car. Something like a fire-red convertible BMW. Or maybe even a limo like the car my mother rode in every day. That was one thing the judge had going for her. She could rock that ride. Just sat back and let Jimmy do the driving.

That's how it was going to be for me. I was going to have a driver. And a stylist. And a makeup and hair team. I was gonna have it all!

On the 212, Aaliyah and India squeezed into one seat, and Veronique and I sat across from them. I was glad to have my main girl to myself.

"I've got something to show you." I pulled Jax's card from my wallet.

Veronique frowned. Turned the card over, just like I did when Jax gave it to me. "What's this?"

"Jax's business card," I said, feeling really proud. "He wants me to call him. But the thing is, I don't have any idea how. He didn't give me his number."

"He forgot to give you his number?"

"Nah, that's not it. He did that on purpose. That's one of the things that makes him so sexy."

"Sexy? That sounds stupid to me."

"Why you always hatin' on Jax like that?"

When Veronique bit her lip, I knew I wasn't going to like what she had to say. She did that every time she was trying to hold back. "I have something to tell you." She took a breath. "Jax is seeing Jayde Monroe."

It felt like she hit me in my stomach. "No, he's not!" Even when I said that, I remembered Jax and Jayde in the gym, fighting like they *were* boyfriend and girlfriend. But I was sure that they weren't, because Jax would have told me. And if he hadn't, Jayde would have said something. That's just the way females were. "He's not with Jayde," I said again, really sure that I was right.

"Word at school is, they are."

"Well, word at school is wrong. Maybe they were together at one time, but I can tell you for real that they are not together now. Trust that."

"So you know for sure that he is not with Jayde?"

"Didn't I just say that?"

Even though I gave her attitude, that didn't stop Veronique. "How do you know?"

" 'Cause if he was with her, he wouldn't be hittin' on me."

"He wouldn't be hittin' on you?" Veronique's eyes got as wide as quarters. "You're kidding, right?"

"No!"

It must have been the way I said that—like I wanted to slap her—that made her back down, although I knew that Veronique was not afraid of me. If there was anyone I didn't want to get into it with, it was Veronique.

She said, "Okay, if he's not hanging with her, then cool. Go for it, my sistah. But all I'm sayin' is be sure. I'm tryin' to keep you away from the drama."

I shrugged. "No problem. I'll ask him just to show you."

"Good."

"Great." I turned to the window, not feeling like talking anymore. That seemed to be just fine with Veronique. She stuffed the MP3 earplugs into her ears and tuned me out.

I was so mad; she'd taken all of my happy away with that nonsense about Jax and Jayde.

I peeked again at his card. How was I supposed to get his number? I needed to get it for real now 'cause I had to talk to him. I had some questions for him, and he needed to give me some answers so that I could prove my girl wrong.

I was so sick of Veronique and Aaliyah. I couldn't wait for the day when both of them would have to say that they were wrong. And when that day came, I was going to make them say that they were sorry, too.

ou don't want to hang?" India asked.

I looked down over the church's balcony and searched for my father in the crowd. I had to find him. "Nah, I can't hang today."

"Too bad, I was thinking we could go to Fridays or maybe catch that brunch at that new place on LaCienega. Sure you don't want to come with us?" India pushed.

"Next time. I gotta get home today."

"For what?" Veronique looked at me as if she knew I was up to something.

"I . . . I want to study."

Now it was Aaliyah's turn to interrogate me like she was the judge. "What are *you* studying?"

"Dang, can't a girl just go home to study? With the dance team and our rehearsals, I need some time to catch up."

Aaliyah shrugged. "Ain't nothing but a thang." Then she turned to India and Veronique as if I wasn't there. "We're gonna catch the bus?"

I watched my crew walk away, and I almost wanted to run after them. But when I thought about what I had to do, I forgot all about my girls. I needed to find my father so that I could get home.

Twenty minutes later, I was in my bedroom in front of my computer. My dad was in the family room, stretched out on the couch watching football. In a few minutes, he'd be doing more sleeping than watching, so he wouldn't be in my business. Not that my dad spent much time doing that. That was the judge's job. But my mother had stayed at church for the second service, which was just fine with me. I'd be able to be in my room without anyone stepping in on my privacy.

With just a few clicks, I was done. I thought it would take hours, but it took less than ten minutes on the Internet. There were nine Xaviers listed in the online directory for Los Angeles. I jotted down the numbers, then lay back on my bed.

I dialed the first number, and after a couple of rings, I heard, "Xavier residence. What's up?"

My whole life I'd been told that there was no such thing as luck—only God's divine intervention. I never knew what that meant—until now. What were the chances of me finding Jax with the first call? This had to be a sign—maybe even a sign from God. Jax Xavier was going to be my boyfriend.

"May I speak to Jax?" I asked, even though I knew it was him.

"Who's this?"

"Diamond."

"Hey, you." He sounded glad to hear from me. "What took you so long to call?"

"First of all, it's not like you gave me a number. And second, I didn't want to call right away because I don't want you to think I'm chasing you. You need to know that I don't chase anyone," I said, making it plain.

"Whoa, girl."

The way he laughed, I knew I'd nailed it. Everybody was always talking about me needing to put down my magazines, but there was a lot more than fashion inside those pages. What I'd just told Jax—I'd read that in a *Cosmo* article. It had worked for the girl in the magazine, and now it worked for me.

"So, you don't chase anyone, huh?" He was still laughing. "Well that's too bad, 'cause I want you to chase me. Chase me and catch me."

He did it again. Gave me that tingling feeling.

"Well," he said, "if you won't chase me, I'll just have to come after you."

I wish you would, I said inside. But aloud I said, "Do that if you want."

He laughed again. "I like you, girl. You got flava. So, how do you like the dance team?"

I leaned against my pillows and imagined Jax lying on the bed with me. Not doing anything because I wasn't that kind of girl. But I could imagine us just lying next to each other as we watched TV, or DVDs, or just listened to music. "I love the dance team. Can't wait for basketball season to start."

"Me neither. This is my big year. Lots of college scouts coming out, so I've got to light up the court and stay healthy."

"You think you got a shot at the pros someday?"

"Yeah, I'd like to go now. But you know you can't go pro from high school anymore. I've got to spend at least a year in college."

"I didn't know that. Where're you going?"

"Got it narrowed down to Georgetown, North Carolina, or Kansas."

"No Black colleges?"

"Nah. My dad went to Hampton, but Black schools ain't good for going pro. So, where are you planning to go?"

I wanted to give him a brilliant answer—a great school and a grand reason for going there. But it wasn't like I'd thought about college all that much. "I'm not sure. My brother's a freshman at Morehouse; that's where my dad went. My mom went to Howard. I may go to Spelman."

"I heard that's a good school. But it's all girls, and I can't imagine a cutey like you hanging with just females."

"Why not? An all-girls school is where all the boys will be hanging out."

"True dat. So how're you getting along with the girls on the dance team?"

I wondered why he would ask me that. And then I wondered if it had something to do with Jayde.

"I get along with everyone fine. Although I have my own crew. I'm not looking to make friends."

"Cool. Have you told your parents about me?"

He was all over the place with his questions. "What should I tell them about you?"

"Well, you could tell them that I'm a nice guy."

"Yeah, you *seem* to be nice, but I don't know you like that."

He laughed. "See, that's why I like you. You're a cutey. You're smart. You got spunk. Did I miss anything?"

"And I'm very mature."

"Oh, yeah? How old are you anyway, fifteen?"

I hoped he wasn't going to hold that against me, but I couldn't lie and say I was older. Then he'd think I'd gotten left back in school. "Yeah, I'm fifteen, but I don't do the things that ordinary fifteen-year-olds do."

"Really?"

"Yeah, you should know that, just by the fact that I made the varsity squad."

"True dat. So, what are the things Diamond Winters likes to do that makes her so mature?"

"A little bit of everything. Go to the movies, hang with my crew. I'm really into fashion."

"I can tell. You want to be a designer or something?"

"Nah, I'm 'bout to become a singer. My girls and I have formed a group." I told him about the Divine Divas, emphasizing all the parts that I knew would impress him.

"Dang, girl," he said when I finished. "You really are going to be a star. Are you going to be on TV?"

"Yeah, when we make it to the finals."

"You know what, Diamond? I like you."

That tingling feeling came back. "I like you, too."

"Good. Then we don't have to do all this chasing and catching stuff. Let's go to the movies."

"Really?"

"Yeah. Let's go this week. Friday night."

"Okay."

"I'll holla at you."

"Okay," I said. But he had already hung up, not even hearing me. I clicked off my phone and jumped off my bed.

I had a date with Jax Xavier. How cool was this? I opened my phone to call Veronique, but then I stopped. With all the stuff she'd said to me, I wasn't sure if I should share this with her. She would ask me lots of questions about Jax and Jayde.

I didn't have to ask Jax anything about Jayde. He'd just asked me out. This proved that he was a free agent.

I'd told my girls that I was going to be studying, and that would have been good—if I could have done it. But I couldn't think about schoolwork right now. I only had a week before my date—to plan what I was going to wear, what I was going to say. But I also had to come up with the most important part of the plan, and that was how I was going to go on a date without my father and the judge finding out.

I grabbed my five new magazines that had just come in. Homework could wait. I had a lot of research to do!

$\mathcal{I}$ loved the way Veronique played the keyboard.

I think she was an example of what people meant when they said you had a gift from God. Veronique had never had a piano lesson in her life, but she played like God had given her the lessons Himself.

Veronique thought she got all of her talent from her dad. That's what she'd told me a few years ago. She didn't really remember her father—I think her mom and dad divorced when she was just two. But she did know that he was some kind of musician who'd left the country to live in France.

Wherever she got her talent, my girl could rock a keyboard. Even when she was just fooling around and making up songs, like we were doing now, Veronique sounded like she should be signed to a recording contract.

"Dang, Vee," Aaliyah said. "Instead of working in the bookstore, you should have tried to find a job playing."

"Wish I could. Maybe one day."

With the way everyone was laughing and feeling good, I decided this was as good a time as any to tell my girls my news. I didn't prep them or anything. I just said, "I have a date with Jax."

I don't know what happened, but the rec room became so quiet, I wondered if anyone was still breathing.

India asked, "Your parents are actually going to let you go out with him?"

"Well, that's the part—"

"Get out," Aaliyah said before I could finish. "Your parents don't even know, do they?"

See, that's one of the problems with hanging with a crew. They knew me too well. "No, I can't tell them; you know the judge's rules. But how can I wait a year to date Jax? He's a senior; he'll be gone by the time I'm sixteen. And if I can't go out with him now, he'll just move on to someone else." When none of them said anything, I added, "I don't want him to think I'm a baby."

"So how are you going to pull this off?" Aaliyah asked.

The way she stood, with her arms folded, I knew she was just waiting to poke all kinds of holes in my plan. But this was one time when I couldn't wait to hear what she had to say. I needed to know every single thing that could go wrong, and Aaliyah could help me better than anyone with that. Her mind worked like a parent's.

"Well, for me to pull this off, I'm gonna need my sisters. I'm gonna need y'all to cover for me."

"And how are we supposed to do that?" Aaliyah asked.

"Here's the plan." I paused, hoping to see at least one of them look as if they were on my side. But none of my girls were feeling this . . . yet. "I'm gonna tell my parents that we're having a sleepover. And they'll believe me, 'cause we've been practicing so much; they know we spend a lot of time together."

No one said anything.

"And you know," I continued, "we could really have a party. I'll just get there kind of late. . . ."

Aaliyah said, "That won't work, because if we have a party at my house, my dad will be there and he'll never let you come in late. And not only that, he'll be sniffing around trying to figure out what's up. You know him. He knows every little trick we have."

That was the truth. It wasn't the greatest thing having the deputy chief of police as your father. He was good for protection, but Mr. Heber always looked as if he knew what was on the mind of every teenager in America.

So Aaliyah was right—her house was out.

India said, "We won't be able to do it at my house either. I've got the same problem as Aaliyah. My mom and dad will be home."

"Come on, guys," I begged. "Help me think of something.

"I'll do it." Veronique rescued me. "But first, I want to know one thing. Did you ask Jax about Jayde Monroe?"

I couldn't believe Veronique went there—asking me that in front of India and Aaliyah. They already had their doubts about him. Her question would just make it worse.

"What about Jayde Monroe?" India asked.

I had to put a stop to this. "Yes, I asked him." It wasn't often that I lied to my girls, but I knew they would never leave this alone until they were sure that Jax was for real. "And he told me he's not seeing her."

"Are you sure?" Veronique asked.

"Yes, that's why he asked me to go out with him."

"Okay, my sistah. If he's not seeing her, then I'm with you. You can tell your parents that you're spending the night with me."

"I don't think this is such a good idea," Aaliyah said in her parental tone. "Something could go wrong and then you'll both be in trouble."

But Veronique ignored her. "My mom will be working till midnight on Friday. So as long as you get there before then, you're cool."

"I'll be there way before midnight."

"Then I got your back. But remember, once my mom gets home, if you're not there, you won't be able to come in. 'Cause if my mom finds out, she'll put a fast stop to all my fun."

"I promise I'll be there." I hugged Veronique. "Thanks, girl."

"Just for you, my sistah."

"I can't believe you're gonna do this," India said.

Veronique shrugged. "I've got to look out for my girl. You never know—I might need her to cover for me one day. And that's what sistahs are for."

"Just be careful," Aaliyah said, looking at both me and Veronique. "This could lead to big trouble."

I knew her warning was meant mostly for me.

"The only trouble we'll get into is if any of us says anything." I looked at Aaliyah and India and begged them silently not to say a word.

"I don't like it, but I'm not gonna give you up," Aaliyah said.

I looked at India.

"Me neither," she said in her quiet way.

My happy was all the way back. I had a plan and I had my girls. And I knew they had my back.

12

Hey, it's me," Aaliyah said.

"Hey, girl." I tucked my phone under my ear and handed the money to the cab driver. "I'll be right back," I whispered and grabbed my bag.

"The meter's running," the driver said.

I jumped out of the car. "What's up?" I asked Aaliyah.

"Nothing. Just wanted you to be careful tonight."

"I will." I had to move quick. I rushed up the stairs in Veronique's apartment building. "But it's not like I'm doing anything. We're just going to the movies."

"I know, but I just want you to know that I got your back, too."

This was why Aaliyah was my girl. She tried to play hard, but she was such a softie. I knew this was her way of saying she was sorry for all of the grief she'd given me about Jax.

"Don't worry about me. I'll call you when I get to Vee's tonight."

By the time I shut my Sidekick, I was already on the third floor and out of breath. I banged on the door, and when it opened, I said, "Hey" before I realized that it wasn't Veronique. Instead, it was one of her little brothers. I could never remember all of their names, so I just said, "Hey" and pushed past him. "Vee!"

She rushed from the kitchen, shocked to see me. "How did you get in?" Then she looked at her brother. "D'Andre, did you open the door?"

He grinned and scooted past us before Veronique could swat him.

"I can't believe he did that," she said, taking my bag from me. "Did your mom drop you off?"

"No, they weren't home. I wanted to leave before they got there. I took a cab."

Veronique looked me up and down. "I can see why."

"What?" I looked down at my denim miniskirt and leggings. Yeah, the skirt was really short, but being the fashionista that I was, I had to be serious with my style. It wasn't such a big deal, since I had on the leggings. "What's wrong?"

"Nothing. You look cute. You just better not run into anyone from church. Or anyone who knows your dad or the judge."

Dang. I hadn't thought of that. Everybody in L.A. hung out at Magic Johnson's Theatre. Especially on Friday night.

"So, you're ready for this?" Veronique asked.

"Yeah, I'm excited."

"Okay," she said. "Don't forget, you need to be here before midnight. Eleven-thirty to be safe."

"I'll be here, I promise." I walked toward the door, but Veronique called me back and hugged me.

"Be careful, my sistah."

Why did my crew keep saying that? Any minute, India would be calling me saying the same thing. Didn't they get it? There was nothing to worry about.

By the time I dashed back down the stairs and into the

cab, the meter was already at seven dollars. Dang. The cabs were going to take all my money. But it wasn't like I had a choice. It wasn't like I could've had Jax pick me up at home. See, this was why I needed my own car.

"Drop me off at Crenshaw and Martin Luther King."

"The mall?"

"No," I said, letting him know that I would never go there. The Beverly Center was more my style. "Drop me off at the movies."

I flipped open my compact, checked my makeup, then sat back in the cab. It was hard to stay calm when all I was thinking about was that in just a few minutes, I was going to be on my very first date.

As soon as I came around the corner, I saw Jax. Just like in school, he was surrounded by an entourage, and I knew he had to be kidding. He didn't plan on having his boys sitting in the movies with us, did he?

But the moment Jax saw me, he swatted at his boys like they were flies. And like flies, they flew away.

"Hey, you." He looked me up and down.

I could tell that he liked what he saw. I liked what I saw, too. Jax was so cool in his jeans and T-shirt. And then to top it off, he had on a pinstripe jacket that could have been part of one of his father's suits. He had style, too. Just another thing we had in common.

He leaned over, and when his lips touched my cheek, I prayed that he wouldn't feel how hot his kiss made my face.

"What's up," I said. I knew I sounded calm and cool, even though I was so far from being collected.

"I must really like you, girl. I don't ever come to the movies this early."

"Well, I'm worth it," I said, keeping up my bold front. I had to give props to my magazines again. Those articles knew how to keep a girl in control.

He took my hand and led me into the theater. I stood with him in the ticket line and thought about how I'd convinced him to go to this early show.

When he'd first said he wanted to meet up at ten o'clock, I'd almost choked. But I'd been quick; I'd come up with a story and he'd bought it.

Jax paid for the tickets and then asked, "You want some popcorn or anything?"

I said, "Whatever you want," thinking that he was such a gentleman. He was the kind of boy my father said he wanted me to have—a gentleman. Over and over, my father told me that he only wanted me to talk to boys who would respect me. "You're special, Diamond," my dad always said. "And you want a boy who will recognize that. A gentleman." Well, Jax was certainly that. My dad would love him.

"So, what time is your practice in the morning?" he asked as we waited at the concession stand.

Even though girls stared and boys stopped, Jax kept all of his attention on me. A gentleman for sure.

"Our practice is at nine," I said, sticking to the lie that I'd told him. "Sorry you had to change your plans, but I can't be out too late."

"It's all love." He handed me a soda and small popcorn, and when I followed him into the theater, I got that tingling feeling again.

But the moment I walked into that darkened room, those special feelings went away. Instead, all I could think about was Veronique. And what she'd said. Suppose someone from church busted me? And the church people weren't my only problem. Almost everybody in the city knew either my mother or my father or my mother and father. Suppose I bumped into one of their friends? Or someone they worked with?

The movie started, and I slid lower in my seat. It was dark, but I still wanted to hide. And then came the moment I'd been waiting for all week—Jax put his arm around me. But instead of leaning my head back on his shoulder like I practiced in my dreams, all I wanted was to shake him away—just in case someone saw us.

"What's wrong?" he whispered.

"Nothing."

But everything was wrong. I wasn't enjoying one minute because every second I was looking over one shoulder, then the other. Looking around to see who was looking at me. I sipped my soda, ate a little bit of popcorn, and did a whole lot of worrying. I prayed for the movie to be over.

It was almost ten o' clock when God granted my wish and the lights came on. I wanted to dash out of that place, hop in a cab, and get to Veronique's house as fast as I could.

"So," Jax began, "how'd you like that?"

We were outside, but I didn't feel any better. "It was alright. I'm not really into all of that shooting and stuff."

"Ah, so you're one of those girls who likes chick flicks."

I shrugged and looked around. I didn't want to talk out here, out in the open. The parking lot was even more crowded than when we'd first gotten here, and everybody who walked by took a second look at Jax. I would have been thrilled—if I hadn't been so obsessed with someone seeing me.

Jax said, "So, you wanna go over to Fatburgers or Starbucks?"

All I wanted to do was get to Veronique's house.

He continued, "I know you have rehearsal in the morning, but it's still early." Then he leaned closer to me. "And I want to spend more time with you."

That should have made me happy, but all I could do was look around the parking lot. Then I wondered if I was being too paranoid. No one was going to see me. I mean, didn't like ten million people live in L.A.? What really were the chances of me seeing someone I knew?

Still, I didn't want to push it. "Okay, I can hang for a little while." I peeked at my watch. "Maybe for an hour," I said, rubbing my throat. "Remember, I have to sing in the morning."

" 'Kay," he said. He put his arm around my waist and led me through the parking lot to his car. It wasn't anything special—just a Honda. But it was *his* Honda. I could get with that.

He opened the door for me—a gentleman—then slipped into the driver's seat. He hooked up his MP3 player and put Jay-Z on blast. With the windows down, everyone we passed scoped us. But I wasn't worried anymore. It wasn't like anyone I knew was cruising down Crenshaw on a Friday night.

Jax drove with one hand and leaned on the console with the other. All the time, he bobbed to the beat. He was so cool, and I imagined spending every weekend this way. I was going to have to convince my parents that I was mature enough to date Jax. I mean, they could trust me; they had to know that.

"So, what you thinkin' 'bout, girl?" Jax yelled over the music.

"Nothing," I shouted back.

He turned down the volume. "That was the wrong answer. You were supposed to say you were thinkin' 'bout me."

"If I was, I wouldn't tell you."

He laughed, turned the music up again, and went back into his world. I leaned into the seat, closed my eyes, and went into my own space. A place where I was with Jax every day. Where we hung out every weekend. Where we rolled through the city in his car. Maybe not this Honda. Maybe something like a fire-red convertible BMW.

I opened my eyes, and now I dipped my head to the beat. I had never, ever felt so grown up.

All of the confidence I had on the ride over went away as soon as we walked into Starbucks. What had I been thinking? This place was high risk. Maybe no one from church would be at the movies this late on Friday, but Starbucks—everybody in Los Angeles hung out here.

I followed Jax inside, all the time looking around, making sure there was no one there I knew.

"What's wrong with you, girl?"

"Nothing."

"You sure, 'cause you don't seem to be having a good time."

"I am. I'm just worried about doing all this talking when I have to sing tomorrow. You know I'm the lead."

He looked surprised. "For real? You didn't tell me that."

"Yeah, so I have to preserve my—" I stopped. And stared. At my next-door neighbor, who'd just walked into Starbucks a few people behind me in the line. "Oh, no."

"What?"

"I have to go to the bathroom."

" 'Kay. What do you want me to get for you?"

"Just water," I whispered before I ran away.

I locked myself inside the single bathroom and walked back and forth, trying to figure a way out of this. My chest ached; surely, I was about to have a heart attack. But anything was better than having to face Mrs-Didn't-Know-How-To-Mind-Her-Own-Business Bower.

From the time I was little, our next-door neighbor had had it in for me, telling my parents everything that she ever saw me do. My brother and I used to think that she was the judge's paid spy—always at her window, always trying to catch me in something. Well, tonight, I was caught.

"Did she follow me?" I asked myself out loud.

I shook my head. No. This whole thing had me really caught up. I needed to calm down and stay in the bathroom long enough for her to leave.

"Hey," someone banged on the door.

I held my breath until they banged again.

"I'm in here," I said, as if that wasn't already obvious.

"I know you're *in there*," a woman shouted. "I've been waiting *out here* for a while."

"I'll be out in a sec."

"Hurry up. Other people need to use the bathroom, you know."

I looked in the mirror one last time and wished that I was anywhere but here. I slid open my Sidekick and called for a cab.

"Twenty minutes!" I yelled when the dispatcher told me that's how long it would take. I could be dead by then if Mrs. Bower was still out there. "Okay." I told them to hurry and that I would meet the cab right outside Star-bucks.

Then I stepped outside the bathroom. I didn't care about the three girls who were lined up against the wall. I didn't care about the way they rolled their eyes. Or the way they sucked their teeth. I only cared about Mrs. Bower. And if she was still out there ready to take me down.

I peeked around the corner.

"Girl, what are you doing?"

I'd almost forgotten about Jax. "I was looking for you," I lied.

"I was about to come looking for *you*."

"I was in the bathroom." I rubbed my neck. "My throat feels kind of sore."

"Really?" He seemed concerned.

I glanced around the coffee shop, and when I didn't see Mrs. Bower, I sat down with Jax. "Yeah, I need to be getting home."

" 'Kay, if you don't want to hang with me."

"It's not that. It's just I have to be careful with my voice. You know when we win this, we're going to get a recording contract."

"Really? That's dope. And as the lead, you'll probably spin off one day and get your own deal."

"Probably." I loved the way Jax looked at me now. Like I was already a star.

"Girl, you gonna be famous."

"I know." I looked at my watch; I couldn't believe an hour had passed since we left the movies. I still had about ten minutes before the cab would come, but I wanted to be outside waiting. Didn't want to take the chance of missing it.

He said, "I guess that means you want to go home."

"Huh?"

"The way you keep looking at your watch."

"Well, don't you have to be in early the night before a big game?"

"True dat. 'Kay, come on."

"No, you stay here."

"What? Nah, I've been raised right. No way I'm letting you go home by yourself. What would your parents say?"

If he only knew. "A car's coming for me."

He laughed. "Dang, girl. You're rolling like a star already. I could've dropped you home."

"No problem. I got this."

"What's wrong? You don't want me to see where you live?"

"It's not that. It's just that this is our first time going out. You don't need to know where I live."

He laughed. "Girl, you're something else. So, first time, huh? You say that like we're going out again."

"Oh, we are," I said with a lot more confidence than I felt. But that's what all the magazines said to do.

" 'Kay, so don't I even get a little kiss?" Jax asked when I stood up.

All I wanted to do was kiss him. In my dreams I kissed him all kinds of ways. But I couldn't take that chance. Not like this. Not now.

I said, "Oh, you'll get your kiss. Next time." And then I strolled out of Starbucks. But the moment I was out of his sight, I dashed to the corner and prayed that the cab was waiting.

13

Veronique and Aaliyah were tired of hearing me, but I had to tell India, because she hadn't come to church yesterday.

"It was so amazing," I said, ignoring the way Aaliyah rolled her eyes. "We went to the movies and then we hung out at Starbucks."

"Wow!" India was impressed. "So, are you and Jax like boyfriend and girlfriend now?"

I must've looked ridiculous the way I grinned, but I couldn't help it. "Not on paper. But you know, that's where we're headed."

"That's so cool."

"You left out the part where you almost got caught," Veronique said.

Aaliyah frowned. "You didn't tell me that."

"Yeah," Veronique said. "She saw her next-door neighbor in Starbucks and almost had one of her heart attacks. Seems to me like the whole night was chaotic."

"Don't listen to her," I said, holding up my hand in Veronique's face. "It wasn't like that. Being with Jax was like magic."

Veronique and Aaliyah said, "Oh, brother," together.

I ignored them and said to India, "I had a great time. I loved being with Jax."

India said, "That sounds so romantic."

Aaliyah said, "Hope it was worth it."

"It was. Trust. I spent over four hours alone with Jax."

I was trying not to be pissed. I always expected Aaliyah to take away my happy, but my girl Veronique was supposed to be on my side. Instead, she had to bring up all that other stuff, messing up my story. I didn't care about anything except that I had gone out with Jax and now we were practically going together.

"So, have you heard from him?"

I wasn't even going to be mad. That was just Aaliyah, doing what Aaliyah always did; she was born to give me grief.

"No, but I told him that I was rehearsing with you guys all weekend. So I knew he wouldn't call me." I left out the part about how I'd been texting him but he hadn't texted me back. I'd been upset at first, but all I had to remember was the way he looked at me and put his arm around me. And the way he wanted to kiss me.

"Speaking of your boy. . . . ," Aaliyah said.

I looked up to see Jax strolling toward us, bouncing his ball, his crew following him.

I couldn't wait to show my girls. I waved. "Hey, Jax."

He leaned back, pointed his index finger at me . . . and then kept right on walking. As if he barely knew me. As if we hadn't gone out together.

"Wow," Aaliyah said.

I waited for her to say something else; I waited for any of my girls to say something. But Veronique just plugged her ears with her headphones, and India stared at her lunch as if her plate might disappear if she stopped looking at it.

"He's just with his boys." No one had asked, but I needed to give an explanation. I needed one myself. "You know how guys are when they're with their boys."

"Yeah," was all Aaliyah said. But at least she said something. The way India and Veronique did their best not to look at me made me want to crawl into the ground.

I couldn't believe Jax played me like that. I picked up my sandwich and pretended to be as focused on my lunch as India was on hers, but I couldn't stop peeking across the yard at Jax. He was at a table in the center, where all the athletes sat, surrounded by his boys. But what got me was that there were girls all around him, too. The way he laughed and talked and bounced his ball, I could tell he wasn't thinking a thing about me.

I thought about everything that had happened on Friday. He'd seemed happy; I know I'd been. Maybe it was the kiss. Maybe if I'd kissed him, he'd be sitting next to me right now.

When I looked up again, I wanted to scream. A girl who was on the varsity cheerleading squad had her hands all over him. I wanted to go over there and slap her away even though I knew I couldn't. Jax would think I was crazy. And my crew would stop me before I got halfway across the yard.

But I wasn't about to give up. This was the beginning for Jax and me. I was going to do something—something that would keep Jax's attention on me. Just me. Always me.

I didn't know what that was yet, but I'd figure it out. Once I did, Jax and I would be a couple for real—and for a very long time.

14

Okay, let's try this again from the top!" Turquoise shouted.

The music started playing, and I stepped and moved with my girls. Any other day, I would have loved being here. Learning how to dance with Turquoise was awesome. She could dance better than any singer out there, and working with her was just another reason why I thought we would win.

But it was hard to concentrate when all I could think about was Jax. It had been over a week since our date and I hadn't heard a word from him. What was worse was that every time I saw him in school, he just pointed his dumb finger at me. And then hung out with all those other girls.

"Diamond! What're you doing?"

I looked up and my girls were on the other side of the room. What had I missed?

"I'm sorry."

Sybil said, "Come on now. We've been working for six weeks and we don't have a lot of time left. This is not the time to be half-stepping . . . literally."

"I'm sorry," I said again. "I'm not feeling well."

"What's wrong?" India asked.

I tried to put on the saddest face I could. It wasn't hard—all I had to do was think about Jax. "My stomach's been bothering me all day." It wasn't a lie—my stomach was all twisted every time I thought about Jax.

"You seemed fine at school."

I glared at Aaliyah. "Because I didn't want any of you to know," I said, giving her attitude. "I didn't want you to be worried." I turned to Sybil. "I only came to rehearsal because I'm committed, like you asked us to be. But I'm really sick." I laid my hand on my stomach to really make my point.

Sybil looked at me the same way Aaliyah had done. I don't know why they didn't believe me. It wasn't like I messed up a lot. Or got sick a lot. Or even lied a lot.

"You know what?" Sybil began. "Let's just end it here. We'll get together later in the week, depending on your schedules."

"Thanks, Sybil," I moaned, so that she would think that I was extra sick.

"No problem. But if you want to call yourself divas, especially winning divas, you'd better buckle down."

"I'll be better, I promise."

"Do you think you're up to still seeing my mom?" India asked.

I'd forgotten all about that. One of Ms. Tova's designers had come up with some ideas for what we would wear. I loved the idea of working with a designer—except for today.

"Yeah," I said. "I can still meet with your mom."

But I must've sounded pitiful, because India said, "Let's just look at the designs tomorrow."

That was fine with me, because I couldn't wait to get

home. I had to figure out a way to get me and Jax back on track.

I'd just walked through the front door when the judge said, "You're home early."

"Yeah, Sybil wanted to give us a little time off."

"Good. I've been worried about all the time you girls have been rehearsing. And then with your dance practice, how're your classes?"

"Fine."

The judge gave me the mother-eye, and that meant more questions were coming. All I wanted to do was go to my room, but the judge wasn't having it.

She said, "So, you're still doing okay with balancing your schoolwork and your activities?"

"Yes."

"Dance practice and the divas aren't getting in the way?"

I wanted to scream. Didn't I just tell her that I was doing fine? But if I ever came at the judge that way, she would slap me into next week and dare somebody to come and arrest her for child abuse. The best way to handle the judge was to turn on the charm.

"Sometimes it's kinda tough doing everything. But I've gotten more organized. And I'm getting it all done." For extra effect, I added, "I think my teachers are all happy."

"That's good."

"I just want you and Daddy to be proud of me."

That did it. The judge smiled. "We're already proud of you, dear." That was one of her favorite lines, but I knew my mother meant it.

"Thanks." I kissed her cheek.

"You should be getting the first round of report cards soon, right?"

Dang! Just when I started to feel a little better. The judge really knew how to ruin my day. "Yes."

"Good; have you eaten?"

"Yes," I said even though I hadn't eaten a thing. I couldn't. Not with the way my stomach was twirling. "I've got to study for my biology test on Friday."

"Biology. That was one of my favorite subjects in school."

Of course it was, I thought. Along with English, math, and history. There was not a subject my mother didn't like.

"Are you ready for the test?"

"Yes," I lied. "Is Daddy home?"

"Not yet. He had a late council meeting, but he'll be here any minute. Go on; I don't want to keep you from studying."

"Thanks, Mother."

I dashed up the stairs, but studying wasn't on my mind. Even though my big test was just three days away, I had to do something else first.

I needed some advice. Inside my bedroom, I flipped through my magazines, but there was nothing. Nothing to tell me what to do when the boy didn't call.

Then I had a horrible thought—suppose Jax thought that I wasn't interested in him? When he ignored me in school, I just ignored him back. Just played it off as if he wasn't hurting my feelings. And I hadn't called or sent a text.

I jumped off my bed and checked the hallway. My mother was still downstairs, waiting for my father to come home. That would keep her out of my business for a little while.

I took a deep breath and dialed his number. I was surprised when he answered his cell right away.

"Hey, you."

"Hey, Jax. This is Diamond."

"I know who it is. I have your number saved."

"You do?" It hadn't even taken a minute for that tingling feeling to come.

"Yeah, girl, of course I have your number saved in my cell. Why wouldn't I?"

I wanted to ask him why—if he had my number—hadn't he used it. But instead, all I said was, "I was calling . . . to thank you for the movies."

"No prob. I had a great time with you."

"You did?"

"Yeah, I can't stop thinking about it."

"You can't?" I hoped I didn't sound as silly to him as I did to myself. It was just that it felt good to know that he felt the same way I did.

"Nah, I can't stop thinking 'bout you. You're special, Diamond. You're really different. I could really like you."

I pushed my face into my pillow so that I could scream without him—or the judge—hearing me.

"Plus," he continued, "you're about to be a star! And that's who I want—a star. How's that singing stuff going anyway?"

"We're doing good. We had rehearsal tonight."

"Oh, yeah? So you're in this group with Aaliyah, Veronique, and that girl India, right?"

"Uh-huh, that's my crew."

"Aaliyah sure is a cutie."

I frowned.

"And Veronique isn't bad either, although she's not my type, with that wild hair and everything. Plus, I'm not feeling her militia vibe, know what I'm sayin'? But she sure is fine."

I could not believe this boy was talking about how cute my girls were.

"But there's no question," he said. "You're the dime. You're the finest one."

My happy was back. He was probably just being polite, talking about my girls that way. He should've said something about India, too. I hated that boys left her out sometimes just because she was a little overweight. But they were the ones missing out, because India was so sweet.

"So," he said, making my attention come back to him, "how many guys have you dated?"

He almost knocked me off the bed with that question. I wasn't sure what I was supposed to say. I thought about my magazine articles, but I couldn't think of anything that would help me with this question. "Why do you want to know?" I asked, turning it back on him. I wasn't a politician's daughter for nothing.

"Because I want to be more important to you than any guy you've ever known."

"Well, the other guys I've known always called me after we went out." I hadn't planned to go there, but I wasn't going to just fall for his lines. Yes, he gave me that tingling feeling, but I still needed to know what was up.

"Sorry 'bout that," he said. "It's just that after we went out, I realized how serious I could be about you. And that bothered me."

"Why?"

" 'Cause I haven't felt this way about a girl in a long time. Maybe even never."

I so wanted to believe him.

"How do you feel, Diamond? How do you feel about me?"

The one thing the magazine articles said was to always be honest. "I feel the same way about you, but I was a little confused when you didn't call me."

"You understand that now, right?"

"I guess." I wasn't sure that I believed him.

"What if I promised that from now on I'll call you every day?"

"Really?" Now he had my attention.

"Yeah. Girl, I'm gonna call you so much you'll be sick of me."

"I would never get sick of you."

"That's what you say now. But we'll see. I'll be calling you before you go to sleep. I'll be calling you to wake you up. We'll see how you feel then." He laughed.

I laughed, too. This phone call was going so much better than I ever thought. I felt like Jax was already my boyfriend. I just had to figure out a way to make Jax want that, too.

"Diamond, can I ask you something?"

"What?"

"Before I ask, promise that you won't get mad."

I frowned, not liking the sound of this. "Get mad for what?"

"For my question. It's just that I want to know everything about you."

"Okay."

I wondered why he was so quiet, until he said, "Are you a virgin?"

I didn't hesitate. "Yes!"

Then it was quiet again. I thought maybe I had given him the wrong answer. But I'd been so shocked by his question that all I could do was be honest.

"I'm surprised," he finally said.

I didn't know what that meant. "Why?"

"Because you're a dime."

What did looks have to do with this? But I decided since I'd told him this much, he needed to know the whole truth. "Well, I'm a Christian and I'm saving myself for my husband."

Again there was that quiet. Again, I thought I'd said too much. But Pastor Ford always told us to be bold in our walk with God.

"Wow," he said. "I haven't heard many girls say that."

"You haven't met many girls like me."

"True dat. Saving yourself. For your husband." He stopped for a moment. "Maybe you're saving yourself for me."

I couldn't say a word because of that tingling feeling again. But this time, it felt different. Stronger.

"Yeah," he said. "Maybe I'll be your first."

I didn't know what to say.

"So," he said softly, "will you let me be your first, Diamond?"

"If you're my husband, you'll be my first."

He laughed. "Well then, we gotta start working on that. Listen, I gotta run, but holla at your boy."

I clicked off my phone, but I didn't want to move from my bed. I wanted to just stay right there and remember everything Jax had said. It was official—we were boyfriend and girlfriend. Kinda. Not that he had exactly said that we were. But he'd said everything else: he was going to call me every day . . . and he wanted to be the first one to have sex with me. On top of that, he was already talking about us being married.

It was happening kind of fast, but I'd read in a magazine that when it was true love, you knew it right away. That's the way it was with me and Jax. We were the truth.

All I wanted to do was think about Jax, but I opened my biology book. I had to get at least some studying done. After five minutes, I closed the book. I couldn't concentrate—there was only one thing on my mind. If Jax was going to be my boyfriend, I wanted everyone to know—even my parents. I was going to have to talk to them. Convince them that I was mature enough to start dating. I was pretty sure that I could talk my daddy into it. But my mother—she was a different story.

I picked up my Sidekick and pressed the speed dial for the one person who knew exactly what I needed to say to the judge. My brother had been through this kind of stuff with our mother. He'd give me some tips.

But my call went straight to his voice mail.

"Hey, it's Diamond. Hit me back as soon as you can. It's important." I stopped, ready to hang up. But before I did, I added, "And this is not about money!"

I clicked off my phone. Couldn't have my brother thinking that I was hitting him up for some dollars. No, this was much more important, and I had to make sure that he would call me back.

$\mathcal{I}$ couldn't believe it. Couldn't believe that I'd waited until the night before to study for this biology exam. It wasn't totally my fault. I had planned to get started last night. But I'd gotten in from dance practice after seven, and then, just like he'd said, Jax had called around eight, and we talked until the judge had come knocking on my door.

I had been so embarrassed when she'd interrupted us. "Diamond, are you on the phone?"

Dang! I hadn't even heard her coming. "Hold on a sec, Jax." I had tucked my phone underneath my covers and put my biology book on my lap. By the time my mother had crashed into my bedroom, I'd looked like I'd been in full-fledge study mode.

"No, Mother. I'm not on the phone. I'm studying."

My mother had given me the serious mother-eye, like she'd known I was lying. I'd prayed that she wouldn't say anything stupid, because Jax had been able to hear everything. "I've told you about studying on your bed. You'll work better at your desk."

Normally, I would have tried to convince her that I was just fine where I was, but all I'd wanted was for her to get out of my room. So I'd jumped up and sat at my desk.

I'd smiled at my mother, but she hadn't smiled back. She'd known something hadn't been right, but thank God, she'd left me alone.

I'd waited a couple of seconds before I'd dashed back to my bed. "Jax, are you still there?" I had whispered into my phone.

"Yeah, girl. What's up with that?"

"It was just my mother," I'd said, keeping my voice low.

"Oh, so you can't have phone calls late?"

I hadn't wanted him to know that my parents treated me like a baby. "Nah, it's not that. I can have phone calls any time I want."

"So, why are you whispering?"

I had looked around my room real quick and eyed my walk-in closet. Inside, I could speak with a normal voice. "It's just that I have a biology test on Friday," I'd said after I'd been safely hidden from my mother. "And you know how parents are. My mother wants me to get all As."

"She's one of those, huh?"

"Yeah," I'd said. I had stayed hidden in the closet, talking to Jax until so late last night that all I'd been able to do was crawl into bed and dream about him.

Now, tonight, I didn't have any choice. I had to crank up the studying. I was glad that on Thursdays I didn't have dance practice or rehearsals. I could just focus. And I had to, because now it was either do or die.

Just as I opened up my textbook, my Sidekick vibrated. I had turned off Fergie because I never knew when Jax was going to call. I couldn't chance the judge or even my father hearing my phone ring so late.

I glanced at the screen, tossed my textbook aside, and rushed into my closet.

"Hey, Jax."

"Hey, you. Whatcha doing?"

"Nothing. A little studying."

"Oh, I don't want to take you away from that."

"No, I want to talk to you."

"You do, huh?"

"Yeah, I like talking to you."

"So, how am I doing?"

"What do you mean?"

"Calling you every night."

It had only been three nights in a row, but I still said, "You're doing good."

"Does that mean I'm going to get a little reward soon?"

I knew he was flirting and I flirted right back. "What kind of reward do you want?"

"Oh, I don't know. A little something. Like maybe a little kiss. You haven't even kissed your boy yet."

Did I know that! All I could think about—all day, and all night—was kissing Jax. My wish had been that he would have kissed me already—sometime at school. Especially since we were so close now.

But in school, it really wasn't much different with Jax. He didn't point his finger at me anymore. Now he smiled and waved. But he didn't do a thing to let people know that we were an almost-couple.

I didn't feel as bad about it as I had last week because now I knew that he really liked me. It was probably just that stupid image thing that guys—especially the athletes— liked to keep. Jax probably didn't want his boys teasing him, since he was the star and everything.

"So, am I going to get that kiss soon?" he asked.

"Anytime you want it."

"Girl, don't make me get in my car and come over there."

He stopped me from breathing when he said that. He couldn't come over here. I hadn't said a word to my parents.

He must've smelled my fear, even over the phone, because he said, "I'm just kiddin'. I know I can't come over there tonight. You're studying."

"Yeah," I said, taking a deep breath.

"But I'ma hold you to that kiss."

I wanted to tell him that I couldn't wait. That if I could figure out a way, I'd meet him somewhere right now.

"I bet you can really kiss, huh, Diamond?"

"I'm all right." I didn't want to seem too confident since I'd never kissed a boy before—well, I'd kissed Walter Hines in the third grade and then Harry Wilson in the sixth grade. But I couldn't call those any kind of real kisses.

"Girl, you'd better stop it. Or I'm gonna have to come over there right now."

This time, I laughed with him.

"Hey, I got another call coming in. Hit me back in an hour."

"Okay," I said. I glanced at the clock as I hung up. It was already ten-thirty-seven. By eleven, my parents would be in their bedroom, and if I called Jax back from my closet, they would never know. I'd have to be careful though, because if they found out that I was on the phone that late, the judge would ground me forever.

But I wasn't going to let all those dumb as-long-as-you-live-in-my-house rules stop my flow. I'd call him in an hour; I'd just have to be super careful.

I lay on my bed and looked at my biology book. I wanted to study, but I was just too tired. I'd be all right. I was a decent student, and I'd been paying attention in class. It might not be my best grade, but I'd pass. That was for sure.

I closed my eyes, but I wasn't about to fall asleep. I had to be up in an hour to call Jax back. Just like he wanted me to.

16

That's a wrap!" Sybil shouted and clapped her hands. "Now see, that was fierce." We all laughed as Sybil pointed at me. "And it's a good thing, since we're getting close. Just one month and counting."

"I think it's because we met early today," I said. It was a teacher's admin day, set aside for the teachers to prepare midterm grades. That had meant a free day for us. When we'd told Sybil, she'd agreed that we would meet this afternoon rather than this evening. It worked for me because tonight was the first basketball game, and there was no way I was going to miss that. Tonight was my debut—as part of the dance team and as Jax's girl.

"Ladies, today you were definitely divine divas for real. Keep it up. We're almost there."

After Sybil left us alone, I said, "We should hang for a little while. Let's go to the mall; my treat for frappicinos."

"I wish I could," Aaliyah said, "but I'm going with my dad to some event tonight, so I have to handle my homework now."

"You're not going to the game?" I was shocked. I thought everyone would be there.

"Nope. I'm not that big on basketball anyway."

"Yeah, but it's our first game. Against Crenshaw. And everyone says that we have a shot to win . . . because of Jax."

Aaliyah rolled her eyes when I said his name. I ignored her and turned to India and Veronique.

"I can't go either," India said. "My mom is being interviewed today, and I don't know what time we'll finish."

India's life was so cool! Ms. Tova was always being interviewed by some magazine or TV show.

"Who's interviewing her now?" I asked.

India shrugged. "Whoever it is, they want me and my dad there, too."

Now that was a reason to miss the basketball game. If someone wanted to interview me, I might have to miss the game . . . nah! I wouldn't miss this for anything in the world. Not when my boyfriend was the star of the team.

"What about you?" I asked Veronique.

"I have to babysit tonight, but I'm cool to hang for a little while." Then she stopped, as if she'd just thought of something. "You sure you don't want to go straight home since you have the game tonight?"

"I can hang for a little while," I said, even though Veronique was right. I needed to get home, especially since I didn't feel so good about how I'd done on my bio test last Friday. We hadn't gotten our grades yet, so I was keeping hope alive. But I knew that I really had to find a way to juggle school, the dance team, the divas, and especially Jax. I hated, hated, hated to admit it, but it looked like the judge was right. My schedule was tougher to handle than I thought it would be.

So my plan was to get busy on my schoolwork, but first, I needed to talk. In a way, I was glad that India and Aaliyah couldn't hang. This would give me time with my girl. Veronique didn't like Jax, but at least she would listen. And she wouldn't try to take away my happy the way Aaliyah always did.

Fifteen minutes later, Veronique and I were strolling through the Fox Hills Mall, sipping our strawberry frappicinos.

"So why'd you drag me here?" Veronique asked.

"What are you talking about? We always hang together."

"Yeah, we do. But we're sistahs. So I know when it's more than just hanging. Talk." When I didn't say anything, she said, "It's Jax, isn't it?"

"Yeah, girl, it's getting really intense. He calls me every single day. And over the weekend, he called me twice on Saturday and then twice on Sunday."

Veronique slurped on her drink. "So why does he act like he doesn't know you when we're in school?"

I wished my girl hadn't brought that up, but I had to admit it still bothered me. In school, he'd just smile, wave, and then go about his business like I wasn't even a part of his world. And his business included a lot more girls these days. I guess it was because of basketball season. The other girls—the ones who were always hanging all over him—were part of that image that he talked about.

"Well you know how guys are," was all I could say. "He might not act like it in school, but I know he cares about me because you should hear the kinds of things he says."

"Like what?"

"Like last night he told me that when he's not with me he feels like a bird without wings."

"Oh brother."

"You don't think that's romantic?"

"It could be."

"Well, it was. Maybe if you heard the way he said it, you'd believe me."

"I believe you. I just don't believe him."

"But he really means it. I know, because—"

"Because what? Because the words sound so good? Please, anyone can come up with a good line. Tomorrow he'll probably tell you that when he's not with you, he can hardly breathe." She held her hand up to her forehead like she was about to faint and then laughed. (That just made me mad.)

"Why are you making fun like this? I wouldn't do that to you."

It still took Veronique a few seconds for her to stop laughing. "I know you wouldn't. I'm sorry. It's just that I don't know . . . I just don't feel like he's serious."

"Well, he is." I paused, knowing exactly how I could prove it. "He asked me if I was a virgin."

That did it. Veronique stopped walking. Stopped drinking her frappicino. And definitely stopped laughing. "Why would he ask you that?"

"He just wanted to know because he said he wanted to be my first."

"See, that's what I'm talking about." Veronique was waving her hand all in the air. "I don't trust him."

"Why? Because he asked me a question? That's all it was, and I think it's good that he asked. If we're going steady—"

"Diamond, you're not going steady! He doesn't even speak to you in school."

"I told you what that was about."

Veronique looked at me as if I was the most pathetic person on earth. "Well, whatever, you're not going to do anything with him, are you?"

I stared back at her.

"Are you?"

"No!"

"Okay," she said. And then after a moment, she added, "My sistah, just remember, the only way to keep the boy is to keep the boy waiting."

I could not believe my girl was tossing me some line that her mother had probably tossed her. I didn't need any lines. I needed my friend to hear me and to understand how much I really liked Jax.

And anyway, it wasn't like I was going to have sex with Jax. He'd have to treat me a lot better before I would even consider something that big.

We kept strolling through the mall, sipping on our drinks, but I let Veronique change the subject to something she loved.

"I'm really having a hard time trying to decide between senators Barack and Hillary," she said, using the first names of the presidential candidates like they were her friends or something.

"Decide what? You can't even vote."

"That's not gonna stop me from getting involved. I just don't know if I'm going to work on his campaign or hers."

I let her go on about a presidential election that meant nothing to me. If I couldn't vote, I didn't care.

I talked to her as if what she'd said about Jax hadn't bothered me, even though it did. But it didn't matter what she thought. Or what Aaliyah and India thought. Or what anyone in the world thought. Jax and I were going to be together. We were almost there. Once we were official, everyone would see. And after that, who knew what God would have in store for us?

Like everyone else in the gym, I cheered. Crenshaw High called time out, and we ran to the floor, clapping our hands. The roar from the crowd was so loud, I could barely hear Beyoncé. But I still krumped the way we practiced, thrilled to be at this game. The only thing that would have made this better was if my crew had been in the stands watching me.

At the end of the dance, I posed with my hands on my hips and waited to a silent count of five before I clapped and then ran with the rest of the squad to the edge of the court. By the way the crowd whistled and applauded, I knew we were a hit.

On the sidelines, I watched as the game continued. And just like Jax had done through the first half, he dominated the floor. I had never seen a basketball game this close up. On the first row of the bleachers, I had a prime-time view of my very-close-to-being my boyfriend. Jax ran faster, jumped higher, scored more than any other player out there.

Every time Holy Cross came to our end of the court, I stood up, hoping that Jax would look at me. I wanted him to see me and know that his very-close-to-being-his girlfriend was so proud of him.

But he never looked my way. I understood, though. He was so into the game. That's why he was the star.

With just a few seconds left on the clock, Jax dribbled down the court, pulled up at least three feet from the foul line, then scored a three right before the buzzer to give Holy Cross Prep a four-point victory. I jumped up and down like everyone else. This was the first game, but it felt like the championship. Never before had Holy Cross beat a powerhouse like Crenshaw High.

I ran onto the floor with the rest of the dance team and the cheerleaders to surround the basketball team before we sang the Holy Cross Prep school song.

I kept my eyes on Jax as I sang. He high-fived his team players, slapped his coaches on the back. And then the horrible happened—he started hugging and kissing the girls around him. I froze, just watching. But soon, I'd had enough.

All of the magazines said that you had to stake your claim, take what was yours. And that's just what I was about to do.

I pushed through the glob of people, elbowing everyone out of my way. This was not the way I'd planned it, but tonight would be our first kiss. Right here. Right now. Jax was mine and everyone needed to know it.

I got close, but there was still a line of people in front of me, blocking me from my boyfriend. I needed his help to get closer. Standing on my toes, I waved, "Hey, Jax."

He looked at me. Smiled. Waved. And then walked in the other direction.

I stood there with my mouth wide open, watching Jax just walk away from me, with his boys and his girls. He didn't even bother to look back.

I turned around and almost bumped into Jayde and her girls standing behind me. They were staring at me, laughing. Like they knew something that I didn't. I scooted past as if nothing they said or did ever mattered to me.

"Hey, Diamond," Jayde called me anyway. "How'd you enjoy your first game?"

"It was great," I said, trying to sound completely opposite the way I felt. My feelings were so hurt, I didn't know what to do. "I can't wait til the next game."

"Okay, see you in practice tomorrow." And then, she and her girls laughed even more, like I was the butt of some joke. I marched away as if I didn't care.

Inside the locker room, I changed my clothes, packed my bags, and ignored all the other girls, who chatted excitedly about the game or this boy or that one. They were all getting on my nerves.

I pressed the speed dial to make my call. "Hey, Daddy, the game's over."

"Okay, cupcake. I'm on my way. How was your first game?"

"Fine."

"You don't sound fine."

"I'm fine."

"Okay, sweetheart. Meet me in front. I'll be there in less than ten."

I clicked off my phone, then went back through the gym. Jayde, her crew, and a few other females lingered outside the boys' locker room. I knew what they were waiting for—I knew who they were waiting for.

All day, I'd been so excited. Waiting for my first basketball game. Waiting to see Jax play. Waiting for him to see me. But I didn't have any of that excitement now. All of my happy was gone.

It was hard to fall asleep. Not with Jax on my mind. I couldn't figure him out. It was like he was two people. One of him was so nice, called me all the time, and always made me feel so good. But then there was the other one—the guy who always made me feel so bad.

My Sidekick vibrated, and I jumped from my bed.

"Hey, you," Jax said the moment I answered. "Did I wake you up?"

"Nah, I wasn't asleep," I said, crawling back into bed. I tossed the covers over my head.

"Good. 'Cause I wanted to keep my promise and call you. Every night, remember?"

"I didn't think you'd call me tonight."

"Why not?"

"I dunno."

"Well, you were wrong 'cause I couldn't forget my girl. How'd you like the game?"

I was still reeling over him calling me his girl. "The game was good. You were great."

"You were good, too. Hold on a sec." The way the phone went silent, I could tell that he was covering the mouthpiece. I pressed my phone closer to my ear and heard some noise. Like music. And a lot of talking. He said, "You there?"

"Yeah; where you at?"

"Ah . . . I'm home. Watching TV. Anyway, yeah, you were good tonight."

"Really?"

"Yeah, I bet you thought I wasn't looking. But I was watching you. I just couldn't let you see 'cause Coach would have gotten on my case. I saw you groovin'. You were the best one out there."

"I tried."

"Listen, I gotta make this run. I'll holla at cha later."

When I clicked off the phone, I glanced at the clock; it was just after midnight and Jax had taken the time to call me. I didn't have to worry about all of those girls waiting for him at the end of the game. I didn't have to worry about the girls that he'd hugged and kissed. All of that meant nothing. It was just part of him being a star. And I could understand that—since I was going to be one, too.

The real deal was that he hugged those girls, and then he called me. I tucked my phone under my pillow—just in case he called back. I closed my eyes and went to sleep. Happy.

17

When I think of love, I think of you." That was what Jax said to me last Wednesday.

On Thursday, he said, "I hit the jackpot when I met you."

And on Friday, when I found out that I'd failed my biology exam, he'd comforted me with, "Don't ever doubt your intelligence. You're as smart as you are beautiful."

Every night, for the last fifteen days, Jax had called me. And every time, every call had gotten better and better. Like tonight, he'd already called me "baby" so many times, it sounded like my name now.

"So, baby, have you told your parents about your biology test yet?"

"Nah," I said, sitting inside my closet. I talked to Jax so much in here that I'd brought in one of the extra bar stools that my parents had stored in the garage. "I can't tell them. My dad might cut me some slack, but the judge . . . no telling what she'll do."

"You crack me up when you call your mother the judge."

"When you meet her, you'll call her the same thing. Trust."

"So, when will that be?"

"What?"

"When am I going to meet your parents?"

There was no way that was going to happen. Not any time soon, and not after that D I'd gotten on the biology test. In my whole life, I'd never seen a D on a paper, and now that D was going to show up on my report card. I was already trying to figure out how I was going to explain my grades to my parents. I couldn't handle the pressure of explaining Jax to them, too.

"So," Jax said when I didn't answer him, "you embarrassed to have me meet your parents?"

"You embarrassed to have me meet your friends?" I replied. Jax stayed quiet, and in the dark of my closet, I smiled. I knew how to turn a question around for sure. If this acting/singing/star thing didn't work out, I could follow my dad and become a politician. I might not have been on top of it like my girl Veronique, but no one could tell me that I didn't know a little something 'bout politics.

"Who said I didn't want you to meet my friends?"

"You never talk to me at school. Like you don't want anyone to know that we're together."

"Is that what you think, baby?"

He just melted me every time he called me that.

He continued, "You know how it is. I'm a star. There's a certain image I have to keep."

"Well, you always say that I'm a star, too. And with the Divine Divas, I will be one."

"True dat. But it's different for me. I gotta keep a certain profile, you know. Keep the babes guessing so they'll come to the games."

"Is that why you're always hanging around those girls and hugging and kissing them after the games?"

"Yeah, that's all it is. Don't tell me you're jealous."

I told him a big bold lie. "I'm not."

"Good, 'cause it's all about business for me. You know, scouts come to the games when they hear that a team can pack a stadium."

What was he talking about? Holy Cross didn't play in any stadium. All of our home games were played right in the gym.

He said, "I'm doing all of this for my future. And my future is your future. You understand that, don't you, baby?"

What was I supposed to say after that?

"I just want you to know, Diamond, that if I could, I would scream from the top of the school that you were my girl because I really want everyone to know."

There was nothing I could say for sure now. That was the first time that he ever called me his girlfriend. I wanted to scream; I wanted to shout. But I couldn't do either—not sitting inside my closet.

"So, you understand, don't you?"

I opened my mouth, and then froze.

"Diamond!" It was the judge. She was in my room.

I clicked off the phone and tossed it into a pile of clothes lying on the floor a moment before my mother pushed open the closet door. "What are you doing in here?"

"Nothing."

She gave me the mother-eye and I gave her a smile.

"I was just trying to decide what to wear tomorrow," I said, pushing past her. I wanted to get far away from the phone, just in case Jax called back. I prayed that if he did, the clothes would muffle the vibration.

"Were you in there talking on the phone?"

"On the phone? In the closet?" Now I gave her one of *my* looks—I looked at her like she was crazy. "I wasn't talking. I was *singing*. Sybil told us to practice whenever we had the chance, so that's what I was doing."

"Uh-huh." She stared at me some more. "Anyway, here." She handed me a couple of blouses on hangers. "Carmen left these in the laundry room."

"Thanks, Mother."

She gave me some more of that mother-eye before she walked slowly toward the door. She was almost in the hallway when she turned around and said, "It's eleven o'clock," like I needed some kind of time check. And then she left.

Maybe she knew that I was on the phone, but she couldn't prove it. I guess her telling me the time was a warning.

I waited a couple of minutes and then grabbed my Sidekick. I had a missed call—Jax. But I wasn't about to take a chance and call him. Not even inside the closet.

I opened my phone and texted: *GTG CUL8R.* And then after a moment, I added *KOTL.*

I closed my Sidekick, got into bed, and wondered what he would think about my text. There was nothing wrong with giving Jax a kiss on the lips—even if it was just in a text. It was official—I was his girl. So we should kiss.

I closed my eyes, but I didn't sleep. I was awake, but I felt like I was dreaming. Dreaming about Jax. And us. Kissing on the lips. But not in a text. Kissing for real. I wondered how much longer it would be before I would be able to make that happen.

18

It had taken me all day to get enough courage, but I was as ready as I was ever going to be. This entire plan was Jax's idea. He'd given it to me when he'd called this morning and asked me again if I'd told my parents about my bio exam.

"Nah. I'm kinda thinking that maybe I'll just wait until I get my midterm grades. That'll give me some time to come up with a good story."

"That's not the way to do it."

"Why not?"

"Look, I've been in this situation so many times it's not funny. But I always win 'cause I kinda treat it like a basketball game. You ever heard of the saying, 'The best defense is a great offense'?"

"No."

"Well, that just means that you go at your parents before they have a chance to come at you."

"Go at them with what, my grade?"

"Yup."

"You have lost your mind. You don't know my father, and you definitely don't know the judge."

"I'm telling you, I know what I'm talking about. All you've got to do is go to them straight, tell them about the

D, but here's the good part. Tell them that you've already got a plan to fix this. That you've already worked it out. I'm telling you, my plan will work. It always does—even with the judge. Parents like that kind of thing. They like it when you take responsibility."

Responsibility—that was the judge's favorite word. But I still wasn't feeling Jax's plan. Until I thought about it. And the more I thought about it, the more I thought that it might work. My mother always said that if I came to them with the truth, I would never get in trouble. This was my chance to see if *that* was the truth.

I folded my test in my hand, then found my parents downstairs in the family room. "Mother, Daddy, can I talk to you?"

"Certainly, dear."

My mother dropped the paper she was reading, but my father continued working on his crossword puzzle.

"Linden, Diamond wants to talk to us."

Now my father looked at me. He took a puff on his pipe, then smiled. "Is this going to cost me anything?"

"No, Daddy."

I sat on the ottoman so that I could face them. "I wanted to talk to you and Mother about school."

"Is anything wrong?"

I shook my head at my mother. "Not really. It's just that I ran into a little trouble."

Now I had their full attention. "What kind of trouble?" the judge asked. Only she didn't sound like a judge. She sounded worried. And that gave me a little hope.

"Well, when school started, I thought it was going to be easy to keep up, but it's been harder than I thought."

And just that quick the judge was back. My mother

folded her arms and I began to wonder if I'd made a big mistake. Maybe I should have waited until report card time. If I had to be grounded, then later is always better than sooner.

I took a deep breath. "I've been keeping up in all my classes except for biology. We had a test, and even though I really studied . . . I didn't do well."

"What does that mean?" the judge asked.

"I got . . . a D." I opened the paper and showed them. "But I've already started fixing this. I spoke to my teacher, and he's giving me some extra work to make up the grade. And he suggested a tutor I can work with. I've put together a plan so that by the end of the year, I'll be able to get a B." When they didn't say anything, I added, "I wanted to tell you because I wanted to take responsibility."

The quiet kept going. Then my mother said, "I'm disappointed—"

But before she could finish, my dad took up for me. "I have to say, Diamond, I'm glad you came to us."

"Well, I wanted to, Daddy. I wanted to be honest and not have any surprises for you when my midterm grades came in. I thought this was the mature thing to do."

"It was. And I like your plan." He puffed on his pipe some more. "I especially like that you've already taken steps to fix this."

"By the end of the year, you'll be proud of me."

"Well, dear, we're already proud of you," my mother said. "It's just that I'm concerned. Maybe it's time for you to reconsider the dance team."

"No, Mother. I really can handle it. I was just surprised by all the work you get as a sophomore. But I have it under control now."

My dad looked at my mother and said, "You know, Elizabeth, there is such a thing as the sophomore slump."

I didn't know what he was talking about, but if it was going to get the judge on my side, then I was all for it.

My dad said to me, "You're always telling us how mature you are, and to me this proves that you're trying to be."

"Yes," my mother said, although I wasn't sure she really agreed with my father. "It's good that you came to us. But we have to see improvement, Diamond. You'll have to bring this grade up or else we will revisit all of your activities, is that clear?"

"Yes, Mother. And thank you for believing in me." I stood and walked slowly out of the room. But when I got to the staircase, I dashed up the steps. I couldn't believe I'd wiggled out of that! I'd walked right out of the room without being grounded, with my cell phone still on—everything was fine. It was just like Jax had said. My boyfriend was brilliant.

I wanted to call him, but I wasn't going to take the chance, just in case the judge came up here to give me one final word of warning. I bounced on my bed and grabbed my Sidekick: *It wrkd. Ur brilliant. KOTL. CUl8tr.*

I wondered what Jax would think when he read my text. This was the second time I'd told him that I wanted to kiss him. Maybe this time he would get the message.

19

So, you want to kiss me on the lips, huh?"

"Yeah." I was back sitting in my closet. Jax had called really late tonight. Even though it was Friday, the judge had the same rules—no phone after ten. I never could figure out why she didn't give me slack on the weekends. But like she said, as long as I lived in her house, blah, blah, blah.

The lights were off in my bedroom, so I was sitting totally in the dark. Didn't want to give the judge any reason to come sneaking in here. But still, I had to be careful.

It was hard to do that, though, when Jax was saying such wonderful things.

"So," Jax said, "when are you going to kiss me on the lips?"

"I don't know. It's not like we get to spend any time together."

"What do you mean? I speak to you every day."

"Yeah, on the phone, but what about in school?"

The way he sighed made me think I'd made him mad. "I thought you understood that, baby. At school, I have my image."

"Well, what about outside of school? We went to the movies a month ago." I wasn't exactly sure why I said that. It wasn't like I could go anywhere with Jax. My parents still didn't have a clue about him, and I wasn't about to give them one. But even though I couldn't go out with him, he needed to recognize that he needed to pay more attention to me.

"I'm sorry, baby. We do need to spend more time together."

I hadn't expected him to agree with me. "Really?"

"Yeah, we need to take our relationship to the next level."

Okay, I needed to back up a little bit and figure out what he meant.

He then said, "I can't wait to taste your lips."

Although we'd been together for a month, he still made me feel tingly. "Me neither."

"So, you wanna kiss me?"

"Yeah."

"Good, 'cause I can't wait to kiss you." He stopped and then said, "What about something else?"

I frowned. "Something else like what?"

"Something else like making love. What about us making love?"

I was shocked. My eyes and mouth were wide open, but I still couldn't get any words to come out.

He kept talking. "Remember I said I wanted to be your first?"

"Yeah, but I told you. I'm a Christian."

"So am I. Everyone at Holy Cross is a Christian. What does that have to do with anything?"

"Well . . . as Christians, we're supposed to wait until we get married . . . before we have sex."

"Suppose you're gonna marry me? You wanna marry me, don't you?"

There had never been a day like this in my whole life—
a day where so many times in one conversation I didn't
know what to say.

He said, "I wanna marry you."

I really, really liked Jax, but this was moving way too
fast. "I . . . haven't thought a lot about getting married. I'm
too young."

"I'm not talkin' 'bout getting married now. I'm just
sayin', we should get to know each other in every way so
that we can see if we want to get married."

"But that's such a long ways away."

"If you're scared, or if you're just too young, let me
know now, 'cause I'll move on."

"I'm not scared." I didn't want him thinking that I was
just a kid.

"Look," he began. "I really care about you, Diamond,
and I want to show you. Making love is all about showing
someone that you really feel them. That you want to get
to know them on a deep level. And you're the only girl I
want to be with that way. That's how much I care about
you. But if you're not feeling me the same way, let me
know. Let me know right now if you don't care about
me."

"I do care about you. I just don't know if we have to . . .
do that."

"It's what I want, Diamond. What I really want." He
lowered his voice. "Don't you want to do it for me?"

He sounded so sweet, almost like he was begging. Like
he really wanted to be with me. Like he really, really cared.
"I . . . don't know."

"Maybe this is your way of telling me that you're not
feelin' me."

Dang! He sounded so sad now. "I'm not saying that. I love being with you."

"And I love being with you. I may even . . ." He stopped so suddenly.

"You may even what?" I was sitting on the edge of the stool. Was Jax about to say what I thought he was going to say? Was he really going to tell me that he might love me?

He said, "I don't know, Diamond. I've just never felt this way about a girl before. And I was thinking that you'd never felt this way about a guy."

"I haven't."

"So if that's true, then we need to show each other how we feel. I want to show you. Don't you want to show me?"

His words sounded good, but they didn't sound right. All my life everyone told me not to have sex. It was a demand. Like a warning that if I had sex some horrible tragedy was going to happen to me. Besides getting pregnant or getting some disease, I didn't know what else could happen. But I was scared enough not to want to find out.

As if he was reading my mind, he said, "Look, this is scary for me, too. I've never had sex before."

"Really?"

"Nah. I was saving myself, too. For someone I really cared about. For a girl I could imagine marrying. That's you, Diamond." He stopped. "But like I said, if you're not feeling me the same way . . . look, I've gotta make this run. Holla."

Just like that, he hung up. As if we weren't in the middle of the most important conversation of our lives. He just left me to think about everything that he'd said.

Sex. Lots of girls talked about it. Some talked about it all the time, like they were doing it all the time. Even on the news, all of the reporters said that most high school kids were having sex. But not me and my crew. We had all made that vow in church last year to remain virgins until we got married. Last year, that sounded right to me. And honestly, it still felt like the right thing to do, because though I hated to admit it, I didn't really know a lot about sex. It was all over TV and movies, but I knew that stuff wasn't real.

I knew what they taught us in sex education a couple of years back—I knew where everything was inside my body. But really, that was it. The thing was I didn't have anyone to talk to about this. The judge never said a word to me about sex. Not that I wanted to talk to her about it either. And talking to my dad—I'd rather die.

Maybe I needed to talk to my brother about what Jax had said. I mean besides pregnancy or disease, what could be so bad about sex? If Jax and I really cared for each other, was it so wrong?

Of course it was! Why was I even thinking about this? Did I want to have sex with Jax? No! I wanted to be with him, wanted him to be my boyfriend. But I didn't want to have sex with him in order for that to happen.

I climbed into my bed and tried to go to sleep. But it was like my thoughts were people inside of my head. And everyone was talking, giving me a different opinion—about Jax, about all those other girls who wanted to have sex with him, about how Jax only wanted to have sex with me. All of those thoughts made me wonder if I could do this. Maybe I could do it, just for Jax. But in the next minute, I changed my mind again. I could never have sex—not now. I wasn't ready. Right?

Sex or no sex? I just didn't know what to do.

20

This was just not my day. It was hard not to look at my watch as Mr. Berg's lecture went on and on. He'd been talking to me for at least fifteen minutes, which meant I was at least ten minutes late.

"Ms. Winters, I had such expectations for you at the beginning of the semester. You were a good student. But you didn't do well on the midterms, and it doesn't look like your work is getting any better."

All of this just because I didn't turn in my homework.

"It's just unacceptable, Ms. Winters."

"I know, Mr. Berg, and I'm sorry. But I'll make this up. I made up all the other assignments."

"Yes, you did. But you're missing the point, Ms. Winters."

I hated when he called me Ms. Winters. What was wrong with Diamond? But I didn't say anything. I didn't want his talk to last longer.

"All of these late marks will affect your final grade."

"I know, and I'll do much better from now on."

He took off his glasses and wiped his eyes, like I was making him weary or something. "Ms. Winters, you need to be more focused. You're not that far away from the time when you'll have to submit your college applications. And all of these things . . ."

This was when I turned him off. Why was he standing here lecturing me about college? I was just a sophomore. And anyway, I wasn't worried. I was a good student, maybe not lately, but I'd get it together. And I was Elizabeth and Linden Winters's daughter. I was going to college—they'd make sure of it. And really, who knew what was going to happen? With the Divine Divas, I might be a star before I was seventeen. I might not need to go to college.

"So, Ms. Winters, I hope we have an understanding."

"Yes, Mr. Berg. I'll have the assignment tomorrow."

Before he could even nod his head, I was out of that room. Now, because of him, I was probably twenty minutes late.

This was not good. I was doing all right on the team, but Jayde Monroe did not like me. She stayed on my case through every single practice, always yelling, "Diamond, you're not keeping up," or "Diamond, you're out of step." It was always something—even the other girls noticed it. Lucinda, one of the juniors on the squad, was the first one to hip me to the fact that she didn't think Jayde liked me.

"Did you steal her boyfriend or something?" Lucinda asked.

It was supposed to be a joke, and we laughed about it. But Lucinda had no idea how true her question might have been. I'd never asked Jax about Jayde—I didn't have to, since we were a couple now. And he never mentioned her to me anymore. Even if Jax and Jayde had once been together, it was none of my business. All that mattered was that they weren't together now.

So, whatever Jayde's problem was, she needed to get

over it. Because I wasn't going anywhere. I would stay on this squad for as long as I wanted to. It was the only way I could be sure that I'd be at every one of Jax's games.

I dashed around the corner, heading to the gym, and bumped right into Jax.

"Hey, I was looking for you," he said.

"You were?"

"Yeah, I was going to walk you to practice. Thought I might hang out a little and watch you."

My cheeks got fat with my smile. There was just no way to hide my happy when Jax was around. "I'm really late for practice. My math teacher kept me after class."

"Ah, don't worry about it. You're the best on the squad. They'll wait for you."

Of all the days he could have chosen to hang with me in school, why did it have to be today? And why did it have to be now? I loved seeing him, but I needed to get into the gym. "No one in there is going to wait for me," I said, hoping that he would take the hint. "Jayde Monroe will make sure of it. She's not feeling me, and if she had her way, I'd be off the team." I almost asked him if the way Jayde treated me had something to do with him, but when he didn't say anything, neither did I.

"So," he leaned against the wall, as if he didn't care if I was late or not, "you say I don't talk to you in school. But see? Now, I'm talking."

"Yeah."

"And I'm glad to be talking to you. I want everybody to see us."

Okay, maybe practice could wait.

He said, "Have you thought about . . . you know, what we've been talking about?"

A little bit of my happy went away. For the last five nights, that was all Jax had talked about. "I haven't thought about it anymore."

"Why not?"

I shrugged.

He said, "I guess I'm just in a hurry 'cause I'm ready to get real deep with you." He leaned so close to me that I wondered if this was it—was this the moment of my first kiss? "Do you know how much I care for you, Diamond?" he whispered.

It felt like there was a big ole lump in my throat. I couldn't say a word, so I just shook my head.

He said, "I want to tell you and I want to show you how I'm feeling you."

I heard his words, but I was focused more on watching his lips. They were so close to me, I just wanted to push my mouth against his. "Diamond, I really, really think I love—"

"Excuse me!"

I jumped back from Jax.

Jayde's face was tight. She looked at her watch. "Diamond, are you coming to practice, or have you dropped off the team?"

She was talking to me, but she was glaring at Jax.

"I'm sorry. I'll be right in there." I didn't want to be kicked off, but I couldn't leave Jax right now. Not with what he was about to say to me.

"Well?" Jayde stood right there in the hallway as if she had no plan to move.

Why couldn't she just go away and give me a minute? That's all I needed so that I could hear what Jax had to say.

Jax looked back at Jayde, then after a moment, he

laughed and bounced his basketball. "Hey, Dee, you better get in there. I'll holla."

I wanted to beat Jayde down as I watched Jax bounce that ball through the hallway. This was the second time that Jax had come so close to saying that he loved me. And Jayde had ruined it!

I had to hold back as I walked past her.

She said, "If you're late again, you'll be off the team."

I wanted to tell her what she could do with this team, but I didn't. I didn't like her, but I liked the squad. And now, I *had* to be at all of Jax's games. Especially with what he'd just said to me—well, almost said.

I was so excited as I changed into my workout gear. I couldn't wait to get through this practice, and then get home, and then get my call from Jax. He would finish telling me what he'd started. He'd tell me that he loved me. And then, maybe it would be easier. Maybe then I'd be able to do what he was asking me to do. Maybe.

21

I slammed my locker shut, closed my eyes and leaned against it. I was so tired. I had waited all night for Jax to call, but for the first time in weeks, he hadn't. I wondered if this was about me not sleeping with him. I wondered if he was thinking about breaking up with me over this.

"Hey, you."

My eyes popped open. "Hey," I said, surprised and relieved at the same time.

Jax leaned against my locker and bounced his basketball. "You look great."

"Really?" Being the fashionista that I was, I had to add flava to my school uniform every day, even on the days when I wasn't feeling very good. This morning, I'd needed lots of color to try to get my happy back, and at the last minute, I'd grabbed a huge red patent leather belt from my closet that matched my red hoop earrings. I didn't think it was all that special, but now I was glad that I was working this belt.

"You look hot."

It was good to know that he wasn't mad at me. "Thanks." But I still wondered why he hadn't called.

He stopped bouncing the ball. "So, you thought about . . . you know."

"Yeah, I thought about it." I stopped. His boys were always around, and I didn't want anyone to hear what we were talking about. The hallway was filled, but no one seemed to be listening to us. "Jax, I really like you, but I don't think we know each other well enough to have sex," I said, keeping my voice low.

"See, that's the problem, Diamond. You're looking at this as sex. But the thing is," he said as he leaned closer to me, "I don't want to have sex with you."

"But you said—"

"I can hit any female I want." He stopped, pointed at a girl passing by. "I can have her." Then he pointed to another one. "Or her." He turned back to me. "I can have any girl in this school. But the only one I want is you. And I want you, but not for sex." He leaned closer. "I want to make love to you."

The way he looked at me, the way he talked to me, if he had asked me to leave with him right then, I might have.

He said, "This is about love, Diamond." He touched the side of my face, and I melted. "Let's make love, together." When I didn't say anything, he stood up straight and bounced his ball. "I'll hit you later, and then maybe you can let me know if you're feeling me like this."

Before I could say anything, he strolled down the hall, bouncing his ball, like he hadn't just been trying to talk me into sleeping with him.

"Hey, Jax." One of the girls that he'd just pointed to called him.

I watched Jax stop. Point. And then motion for the girl to come to him. She hurried over as if she couldn't wait to get next to him. Jax put his arm around her, kissed her on her lips. Then he turned and looked at me. He winked before they both disappeared around the corner.

"I can't stand him."

My heart was beating so fast that I hadn't even noticed that Aaliyah had walked up behind me. It wasn't until I turned around that I realized India and Veronique were with her.

"I think he's cute," India said.

"He's all right," Veronique added. "In an obvious kind of way."

"You're not still interested in him, are you?" Aaliyah asked.

I shrugged my shoulders. "Nah. I'm so over him."

Veronique raised her eyebrows, but I ignored her.

"That's good," Aaliyah kept talking. "I think there are plenty of other guys who aren't as stuck up as he is."

"Yeah, and anyway, we all need to stay free agents," Veronique said, " 'Cause we're 'bout to be stars. Trust and know, right, Dee?"

"Yeah." I grabbed my workout gear and swung the bag over my shoulder. "I'm heading over to practice. What are you guys going to do?"

"I'm going to the library," Aaliyah said.

What else was new?

"I gotta get home," Veronique told me. "Gotta babysit."

"I'm heading home, too," India added.

"Okay, I'll catch y'all later." I waved to my crew, then rushed down the hallway. Not only was I trying to get to practice but I also needed to get away from where Jax and that girl had been—where they'd just kissed. He'd kissed her; he'd never kissed me. I wondered if he was going to ask her to have sex with him since I wouldn't do it.

"Hey, Diamond," Jayde said when I entered the gym. "Guess you decided to join us on time today. Are you ready?"

"Yeah, I'm ready," I said, already walking away. "I'm ready for a lot more than you know."

"What does that mean?"

See now, she was frowning. She shouldn't have been messing with me. I looked over my shoulder and said to her, "Ask Jax."

I wasn't sure why I went there. But I was so tired of her attitude. I didn't look back again, but I could just picture Jayde's face. Good. It was about time that I stood up to her. I was ready for Jayde. And now I was ready for Jax.

I felt really good as I strolled to the locker room. I'd made up my mind. All I had to figure out was how this was going to play out. All I needed was a time and place.

"Okay, ladies. See you at the game tomorrow night," Jayde said as we wrapped up practice.

I was exhausted, but when I looked up, I got a shot of energy. Because there was Jax. I was so happy that he was waiting for me. Maybe he would walk me home and I could tell him what I decided.

"Hey, Jax," I waved.

But Jax didn't respond. He pointed his finger at Lucinda, and she rushed over to him. I know my eyes were wide as I watched him whisper something in her ear. And it wasn't until Lucinda giggled, grabbed her bag, then walked with Jax out of the gym that I realized my mouth was wide open, too.

It took me a moment to turn around and see Jayde

standing behind me—with the same surprised look that had to be on my face. I didn't look at her as I rushed into the locker room. I could not believe this. What was Jax doing to me?

I grabbed my Sidekick. I had to get my message to him fast. He needed to know my decision before he did anything with Lucinda.

I sent a text to his cell: *Call. I'm ready.*

I waited for him to reply, but after fifteen minutes . . . and nothing . . . I decided to go home. As I walked, I prayed that Jax would somehow see my text. See my message before . . . and then my cell phone rang. I looked at my Sidekick and knew then that God answered prayers.

"Hey, you," he said when I picked up.

"Hey."

"I got your text. So, we're really gonna do this? We're really gonna make love?"

I guess he wasn't with Lucinda if he was asking me that. "It's what you want, right?"

"It's what I really want."

"Then, yeah." I tried to sound excited, but I wasn't. I was more scared than anything.

Jax didn't seem to notice. "Great. This is great, Diamond. So, I gotta game tomorrow, but you wanna go out next Friday?"

"Yeah." I guess Friday was as good as any night. I didn't have a plan yet on how I was going to make this work. It wasn't like I could tell my parents I was staying out all night with a boy. And I didn't even know where we were going to do this—but I guess that part of the plan was up to Jax.

"Then, Friday it is. We went out on our first date on a Friday, do you remember?"

"Yeah."

"And now, this is going to happen on another Friday. From now on, Fridays will be our special night."

"Okay." At least he was starting to make me feel better.

"I promise you, Diamond, we're gonna have a good time."

"Okay."

"I'm gonna make it special for you."

"Okay."

"You don't sound excited."

"I am," I lied.

"Good, because I'm excited, too. We're doing the right thing. We're in love, right?"

Finally. He'd finally said it. "Yeah, we're in love."

"Great. Look, I gotta make this run. Holla."

I stared at my phone; I guess I'd expected just a little bit more the first time he told me that he loved me. But this was okay. He did love me. And now we had a date. A second date. Only this time, it was a much bigger date.

Sex.

But it wasn't sex. I had to remember what Jax had said. Anyone could have sex. We'd be making love. There was a big difference. Maybe it was that difference that made having sex okay. We weren't just two kids doing it. We were in love. And Jax said he was going to make it special. All of that made having sex okay, didn't it?

I sure hoped so.

22

I had three choices: India, Veronique, or Aaliyah.

I chose my girl, Veronique.

I made sure that I was sitting next to her when we stood for praise and worship. In the first service, all of the teenagers hung out in the balcony; not that we were doing anything, we were still in church. But this was our own little space, away from the spying eyes of our mothers.

I swayed and clapped as we sang "Living Right for You, Lord" and just waited for the moment when we would sit down and I could tell Veronique everything that I'd been thinking. Pastor Ford walked up to the altar, and I bowed my head and prayed with the rest of the congregation.

"Turn in your Bibles to Luke, the thirteenth chapter beginning at the twenty-second verse," Pastor Ford said the moment she ended the prayer. "Today, I want to talk about knowing God and knowing of God. There is a difference, you know. And understanding that difference will save you. Repent or perish. That is the message for today."

I had barely found the page in my Bible before I whispered to Veronique, "I have to talk to you."

"Okay," she whispered back. "I don't have to watch my brothers today, so we can go to the mall right after church."

"I have to talk to you now." Veronique looked at me for a moment before she peeked over the railing at Pastor Ford. I couldn't believe my girl was going to ig me like that. But I wasn't having it. I knew exactly how to get her attention. I leaned close to her ear. "Jax wants to have sex with me."

Suddenly, what Pastor was saying didn't seem so important to Veronique. "What are you talking about? I thought you said you were over him."

"I was, but we kinda got back together."

"When?"

"A couple of days ago."

"And he asked you to sleep with him?"

"Ssshhh." I looked around to make sure no one had heard her.

"You're not going to do it, are you?" she asked. I didn't say anything, and that made Veronique slam her Bible shut. "You can't have sex with him," she hissed at me. "He's not even your boyfriend."

"Yes, he is."

"That's crazy. He doesn't even speak to you in school. He hasn't taken you out anywhere since that one fiasco with the movies."

"Well, first of all, I told you that we just got back together. And it's not like I can go out with him in public. My parents don't even know he exists."

"More proof that you don't need to be going to bed with that boy, my sistah. Your parents don't even know."

"Do you think if my parents knew, they'd give me permission? Please. You know the judge."

"And in this case, the judge is right. Jax doesn't care a thing about you."

"You guys better be quiet," Aaliyah warned us from behind. Sitting in front of her was almost as bad as sitting in front of the judge.

For a moment, I did as I was told and focused on Pastor Ford's sermon.

"Luke thirteen shows us that many will knock on the door, calling on the Lord. But few will be let in. You have to decide which side of the door you want to be standing on. You can't just call on the name of the Lord and expect to get in. God is going to want to know what you did and what you didn't do. And if you act like you don't know Him down here, He won't know you up there."

I slid lower in my seat, feeling bad for what I was thinking. And I was a little bit scared. I didn't want God to say that He didn't know me. But sometimes, I wondered if these rules that God set up were too old-fashioned. Like all the rules my parents had about living in their house. I mean, life had changed from those biblical days, just like it had changed from when my parents were young.

I whispered to Veronique, "Jax does care about me," picking up the conversation from where we were before Aaliyah interrupted us. "He calls me every night, sometimes twice."

"Anybody can do that."

"And you should hear the wonderful things he says to me."

"About having sex?"

"No, about being in love with me. He told me that he loved me."

"Oh, brother. All you have to do is read a couple of Hallmark cards to get a few of those lines."

"Why are you hatin' so much?"

"I have lots of reasons, but let's start with the fact that

Jax doesn't really care about you. He just wants to sleep with you."

"That's not true. He really does care. And I think once we make love, he'll care even more."

"Do you know how many girls have fallen for that sorry line?"

"Jax is different."

"Do you know how many girls have said that sorry line?"

"What's the big thing about sex anyway?"

"First, you could get pregnant."

"Like I'm not gonna use protection. Please. I ain't tryin' to have no baby."

"Okay, what about a disease?"

"Vee, look at Jax. Does he look like he has AIDS or something?"

Her eyes got really big. "Diamond, you cannot possibly be that naïve. You can't tell if someone's infected with anything just by looking at them."

"Well, I know Jax is safe. Plus, we're gonna use condoms." When Veronique stayed quiet for a moment, I said, "So, what else you got?"

"What about the fact that we're sitting in church talking about this while Pastor's preaching about people who think they're going to heaven and who are going to find themselves burning in hell. Having sex is a sin."

"No, it's not. God created sex, so—"

"You know what I mean. If you have sex with Jax, that's a sin."

"Sex is not the only sin there is. And anyway, we all sin."

"Pastor says that's the excuse that everyone uses just to keep on sinning."

"Well, it's the truth. If I have sex with Jax, it's not going to be worse than any other sin I could commit . . . or any sin you've committed."

Veronique stared at me for a moment, then opened her Bible. "That's it. I'm done. I don't have anything else to say."

"Cool with me."

Pastor Ford said, "So, you see. Just about everyone knows of God. Just about everyone has heard of Him, some even go to church every Sunday, read their Bibles, and they will tell you that they pray. But they don't *know* Him. They don't have a true relationship. A relationship where they want to be obedient. Want to turn away from sin and turn to Him. I'm not talking about being perfect," Pastor said as she strutted across the altar. "No one is perfect. But when you know God, when you truly know Him, you strive to live the kind of life He wants for you. And if you don't, there will be a price to pay. Remember, even forgiven sins have consequences."

Veronique leaned closer to me. "Listen to Pastor and think about the consequences, my sistah. Because not only is it a big mistake, but I have a feeling that you'll be very sorry."

I shrugged as if I didn't care about what Veronique—or Pastor—was saying, even though I did care. I wanted Veronique on my side. We'd been through so much together, I needed her to have my back. And I didn't want God mad at me, either. I wasn't sure I understood everything I needed to about God, but I knew that He had been good to me and very good to my parents. That's why we had such a fantastic life—at least that's what they told me. But I just couldn't see how God would be upset about this. If He was really God and knew everything, then He had to understand what teenagers were going through in today's times. He had to know how much I really liked Jax and how much Jax really liked me. Why would God want a couple like us to wait to have sex?

When Pastor asked us to stand for the benediction, I stood with everyone else. I loved my girl Veronique, I loved my whole crew. I loved God. But I really loved Jax, and it had come down to this—if I loved him and wanted to keep him, then I had to show him. Even if I didn't really want to do it, I had to so that Jax would know how much I cared.

I did care. And I was ready to prove it.

23

Hi, Mother," I said as I opened the door to my house. I kissed the judge's cheek.

"Hi, Mrs. Winters," India added.

"India, how are you?" My mother hugged her. "You ladies just finishing up with rehearsal?"

"Uh-huh. The four of us got together to practice our steps," I said.

"Yeah, I'm a little slow, and they were tutoring me," India said. "I guess I'm slower because I'm so tall."

"You're not slow." I hated it when India put herself down like that. "You're as good as the rest of us. We all needed to practice."

"I'm sure you're fine, India," my mother said. "I'm sure all the divas are fine. We can't wait to see you ladies perform."

"Mother, can I hang out with India? We're gonna go to the mall, and then I wanted to spend the night at her house." For good measure, I added, "Vee and Aaliyah are going to spend the night there, too."

The way India's eyes got big made me want to scream. She was going to blow my cover if she wasn't careful.

"So, the Divine Divas want to hang, huh?" My mother laughed.

I hated when the judge tried to sound hip. It never worked; she only sounded old to me.

"India, is this all right with your mother?"

"Yes, ma'am."

I thought India was laying it on too thick with that "ma'am" stuff, but I forgot all about that when my mother agreed to let me stay at India's.

"Thanks, Mother. I'm going to pack a couple of things."

I dashed up the stairs, and India followed. Inside my bedroom, I told India that she was the best friend a girl could have.

"I'm only doing this because you're my best friend," India said. "But I don't want to get in trouble."

"Remember I did this with Vee and we were fine. You won't get in trouble, I promise." I grabbed the overnight bag that I had packed last night. "It's not like my mother's going to call your mom or go over to your house. You won't have to do anything else. The judge just has to see me leaving with you."

"I didn't know you were going to say that Aaliyah and Vee were going to be there, too."

"Don't worry about that." I rushed into my bathroom to get my toothbrush. "I've got this all under control."

As I stuffed my toothbrush and toiletries into my bag, I couldn't believe how smart I was. I had planned this whole thing, and I was about to get away with it. *Survivor* didn't have a thing on me—I could outwit, outplay, outlast the best of them. Even my parents! With the way this was going, Jax and I could do this every weekend.

The only thing that made me a little sad was that I couldn't share this with Veronique or Aaliyah. But at least I had India. She was cool; she didn't judge me the way the rest of my crew did. And now that Jax would be my boyfriend for real, Veronique and Aaliyah would have to admit that they were wrong. They'd have to lighten up, and they'd probably even start liking Jax now.

India asked, "Are you scared?"

"To spend the night with Jax? Nah."

"Not just that . . . you know, the other part. Are you sure about this?"

I hoped India wasn't going to start lecturing me like everyone else.

"I'm really sure, India. Jax has been so sweet. I know he'll take care of me. And he's never had sex before, either."

"He hasn't?" she asked like she couldn't believe it.

"No, so that's why I'm not too scared, because we'll be doing this for the first time together."

I didn't want to tell India the truth—that inside, I was terrified. But, I was also excited and was trying to stay focused on that.

"Jax said he's going to make tonight really special. He got us a room at the Hilton and we're going to spend the whole night together."

"That does sound pretty romantic."

"He told me that he's going to love making love to me." When India didn't say anything, I asked her what was wrong.

"I dunno. I like Jax and I'm really glad he's your boyfriend, but . . . we just seem kind of young for this."

"I'm a really mature fifteen-year-old. And anyway, I'm going to be sixteen in a couple of months. In today's times, sixteen is like being twenty. So we don't have to wait for sex anymore. Especially if you're really in love."

I could tell by the way India sucked on her lip that she

had more to say. But the good thing about India was that she kept her opinions to herself—unlike Veronique and Aaliyah, who always took away my happy by telling me every single thought they had.

"Okay, I think I'm ready." I lifted my overnight bag.

"Are you sure about this?"

"Definitely." Before I stepped into the hallway, I looked back into my bedroom. The next time I came in here, I would be a different person. I would be a woman.

Downstairs, I kissed my mother good-bye.

"You girls have a good time tonight."

"We will," I said. Once we were around the corner, I told India, "Don't forget. You can't say a word to anyone. Not even Vee or Aaliyah." Then I hugged her.

"I won't. And you be careful. Hit me if you need anything. I'll keep my cell on all night."

I waved to India, then walked down the hill toward Starbucks, where Jax was waiting for me. I was still scared, but I was a lot more excited. And happy. Jax wanted to be with me. And that was all I needed to know. That thought alone made me feel safe, made this feel all right.

24

Jax opened the hotel room, and I stepped inside. The first thing I saw was the bed. A big bed. And I got scared all over again.

"Baby, we're finally here," Jax said. "I've been waiting for this for a long time."

I tried to smile as he hugged me from behind. It felt wonderful to have his arms around me. But still, that didn't take away my fear.

"Look at this," Jax said as he pushed aside the curtains. "Look at this view."

Although it was dark, it was really pretty. From the fourteenth floor, we had a view of the airplanes lined up, ready to take off from LAX. For a while, we just stood there, looking out the window, watching the planes. Jax held me, and soon I didn't feel the pounding in my chest that had been there since we'd met at Starbucks.

"Diamond, my Diamond," he whispered in my ear. He turned my head and softly kissed me.

I closed my eyes, and it took a moment for me to remember to breathe. Jax was so gentle, and his lips felt so good. Now I was absolutely sure about tonight.

"I have waited a long time to do that," he said.

"So have I."

"Are you hungry?"

"A little," I said. "Are you?"

"I'm hungry for you." He grinned.

I loved Jax. He always said the best things.

"I'm going to order room service," he said.

As he placed the call, I stayed at the window and tried to imagine what the next hours would be like. With the way Jax kissed me, I wasn't scared anymore. I knew that he would take care of me exactly the way he'd promised.

"So, what did you order?" I asked when he got off the phone.

"It's a surprise, but don't worry. I only ordered the best for you." Again, he wrapped his arms around me and I felt safe. My girls had been wrong—I wasn't too young to do this. Not with the way Jax had planned it. I'd heard stories of girls who lost their virginity in the backseat of a car or in sleazy motels. But tonight wouldn't be anything like that. Jax was showing that he cared about me—he'd spent all of this money for this expensive hotel. And now he'd ordered room service. He was showing me that I was worth it. And I couldn't wait to show him that he was worth it, too.

Twenty minutes later, there was a knock on the door, and the room service cart rolled in. I was surprised at the way the guy greeted Jax, like he knew him or something. But my attention was more on the food that Jax had ordered for us. On the cart were hamburgers and French fries and fried shrimp and buffalo wings and quesadillas. It was a feast. It was awesome.

We sat on the bed together and ate. Then we lay back on the soft covers and watched the Lakers play the Phoenix Suns. Jax put his arms around me, and every couple of minutes he kissed me. Even with the Buffalo wings sauce on his lips, I loved the way he tasted. I was having the best time of my life.

When the Lakers won the game on a last second jump shot by Kobe, Jax jumped off the bed and cheered.

"Those are my boys! I'm going to be a Laker one day!"

I believed him. And I was going to be right by his side. Maybe I'd even be a Laker girl. "You're going to be better than Kobe," I said.

With the way he grinned, I knew I made him happy when I said that. "You think so?" He leaned over the bed and kissed me. "You really think I'm going to be better than Kobe?"

"Uh-huh," I said. " 'Cause I think you're really good."

"You do, huh?" He kissed me again. "Do you want to know how good I am?"

"Uh-huh."

It seemed as if he was moving in slow motion, the way he pushed all the plates aside, clicked off the television, and turned off the lights. I closed my eyes when he kissed me. Even though my heart was pounding harder than it ever had, I was excited. And I had never been happier in my whole life.

I lay in the dark with my eyes open. Next to me, Jax snored. I just hadn't been able to fall asleep, but Jax had been sleeping for about an hour.

This had been nothing like what I'd expected. Jax hadn't even given me a chance to put on the new nightgown that I'd bought. And then, it had been over real quick. Like in minutes. And it had hurt—no one had told me about that. All Jax had done afterward was roll over and go to sleep. No hugging. No kissing. No nothing.

Maybe this was just the way it was supposed to be. Maybe guys did this after sex—maybe they needed to rest. It would probably be better when he woke up. He would probably kiss me then. And hug me. I just wanted him to wake up soon.

Jax lifted his head like he heard me thinking. "What time is it?" He rolled over, looked at the clock, then jumped up. "Dang. We got to get out of here. You ready to go?"

"Go? I couldn't remember another time in my life when I'd been more confused. "Go where?"

"Go home."

"Home?" I sat up in the bed and covered myself with the sheet. "I thought we were spending the night."

"Are you kidding?" Jax said, already getting up and getting dressed. "I have to go home. And anyway, why would we be spending the night?"

"But I told my parents that I would be out all night."

"Well then, they'll be glad to see you," he said as he buttoned his shirt.

I was still sitting on the bed without any clothes on.

"Come on, girl. Get up. We have to get out of here."

I couldn't move. It was hard for me to even think. What was I going to do? I couldn't walk into India's house at this hour. Her parents would want to know where I'd been. They would call my parents for sure.

And I couldn't go home. That would be worse.

"Ah, you can go on," I said. "I'll just stay here until morning."

"You can't."

"But you already paid for the room."

"No I didn't! I can't afford a room like this. My boy works here and gave me the hook-up. But we gotta be out by two." He glanced at the clock. "I didn't plan on staying this late. So, unless you've got a couple of hundred dollars, girl, you'd better get movin'."

I rolled off the bed with all kinds of thoughts going through my mind. I slipped on my jeans and top, but I wasn't quick enough for Jax. He kept rushing me, but I couldn't do it any quicker. I couldn't get dressed and think at the same time.

As I got dressed, Jax stayed on his cell, checking his messages. He didn't talk to me, didn't look at me. It was like he'd forgotten all those wonderful things he'd said. If I hadn't been so worried about my parents, I would have been mad. But all I could think about was what I was going to do now.

We were in the elevator before Jax said a word. "Do you want me to drop you home, or do you have another one of your cars coming?"

"I . . . take me home," I said.

I didn't say another word to him; I needed all of my brain power to figure out what I was going to say to my parents when I walked into the house in the middle of the night. This was one of those times when I wished we didn't live in a big house that came with everything—including an alarm.

Less than ten minutes later, we stopped in front of my house. "So, this is where you stay?"

"Yeah." I stared at the house I loved, but it didn't look so good to me now. With all the darkened windows, it looked too big, too scary.

Jax leaned over and kissed me. "Want me to walk you to the door?"

A gentleman.

"No, you don't have to get out." But I didn't get out either. I was too afraid.

"Well, ah . . ."

I could tell Jax was waiting for me to make a move. It seemed to take me forever to get up the nerve to open the door.

"Catch ya later," and then Jax took off.

I was still standing there, right on the edge of the curb, looking at my house. If it hadn't been November, and if it hadn't been so cold, and if I hadn't been so scared, I would have slept in the backyard. But I had to go inside. I didn't have a choice.

I prayed as I walked up the steps. Prayed that tonight, by some miracle, my parents hadn't turned on the alarm.

"Please, God . . ." And then I opened the door.

The alarm blasted so loud, I was sure that everyone on the block was awake now. I punched in the code, but before I could get in the last number, the lights upstairs came on. I heard my parents' footsteps, then saw them standing at the top of the stairs.

"Diamond!" My father rushed down the steps. "What are you doing here?"

"I . . . I got into a fight with India and I wanted to come home."

"At this hour?" It was the judge right behind my father.

"It's no big deal," I said. "India and I got into a fight and I wanted to sleep in my own bed."

"How did you get here?"

I stopped, hadn't thought about that. "I took a cab." But the moment I said those words, I regretted them. It was the look on the judge's face that let me know that that had been the wrong lie.

"Tova put you in a cab? She didn't have the decency to bring you home herself?" The judge stomped into the living room, and I thought I was going to have a heart attack. "I cannot believe her," my mother ranted right before she grabbed the telephone.

"Elizabeth, don't call her now," my father rescued me. "It's too late. Talk to Tova in the morning." Then my father turned to me and said, "If anything like this ever happens again, you call me. I don't want you in any cab in the middle of the night."

"Yes, Daddy." I stopped and looked at my parents. Both of them were angry, but the judge . . . I didn't even want to know what she was thinking. "I wish you guys wouldn't make such a big deal out of this. I'm fine. I'm safe." I paused and added, "Ms. Tova made sure that I got into the cab. The driver was someone she knew." I was so hoping that this lie made the last lie better.

The judge said, "I don't care; she should have brought you home herself."

Seemed like my lies weren't working.

My father said, "Go on upstairs. We'll handle this in the morning."

I couldn't wait to get into my bedroom. My hands were shaking so much. And even though I was exhausted, I couldn't even think about going to sleep. I had to stay awake to come up with something that would keep my parents from calling Ms. Tova. India was going to have to help me.

I peeked into the hallway, and when I was sure my parents were in their bedroom, I called India. But it went straight to her voice mail.

"You were supposed to keep your phone on!" I said, leaving her a message. "Call me as soon as you get this. Trouble!" I hung up, then texted her the same message. There was nothing else I could do until morning.

I lay on my bed, on top of the covers, not even bothering to take my clothes off. Staying dressed would help me stay awake. Then I would call India before my mother got up. India would just have to find a way to keep her mother from the phone.

I was a little nervous about India—Veronique would have been much better at handling something like this. But I'd school India and then pray that she'd be fine.

I lay in the dark, thinking about how this wonderful dream had turned into a nightmare. For the first time, I noticed the ache between my legs. Making love hadn't been anything like I imagined. But at least I'd done it. Now Jax knew how much I cared. We were officially a couple—finally.

I wasn't happy with the way tonight ended, but I guess it wasn't really Jax's fault. There was nothing he could have done if he'd had to be out of the hotel. He should have just told me up front and I would have figured something out. Next time, I would take enough money so that we could stay all night. If I made it through this, we would do it again. Maybe not next weekend, but soon. And next time, we would do it right. Stay all night. And maybe the sex part would be better. All I had to do was get through this tonight and tomorrow. Maybe Sunday. By Monday, hopefully, my mother would have calmed down and wouldn't need to speak to Ms. Tova.

I closed my eyes, but only for a moment. I would wiggle my way out of this mess somehow. I always did.

25

I didn't know where the banging was coming from.

By the time I opened my eyes, the judge was standing over me.

"Diamond, I want to talk to you!"

I glanced at the clock and almost died. How did it get to be nine o'clock? My plan had been to start calling India at six, since my dad left every Saturday at seven for his golf game. But the way my mother was staring me down, I knew there was no need to call India now. My mother knew something—I was just afraid to find out what she knew.

"Diamond, where were you last night?"

As quickly as I could, I tried to think of every single option I had. Tried to go over all the lies I could say, but nothing came to me. "I . . . went on a date."

"A date?" the judge screamed.

I had to talk fast. "Yes, Mommy, and I'm sorry. But I couldn't tell you because you and Daddy don't think I'm old enough to date. But I'm ready to, I really am."

"You're ready to date? And that's why you lied? That's why you come waltzing in here in the middle of the night? Who did you go on this date with?"

"Jax. Jason Xavier. He's the star of the basketball team.

He's in the newspaper every week and he's really nice, Mommy."

"Where did you go?"

The lies hadn't been working very well for me, but I wasn't about to tell the truth now. "We . . . we went to the movies, and then he took me out to dinner." That wasn't completely a lie. It wasn't last night, but Jax had taken me to the movies and then out to dinner—in a way—to Starbucks.

My mother gave me that mother-eye, only it was worse than any other time in my whole life. "Where did you eat?" her interrogation went on.

I wasn't about to tell her Starbucks. "I . . . don't remember the name of the restaurant. It was on Wilshire somewhere. Jax was driving."

"What restaurants are open until two in the morning, Diamond?"

"I don't remember the name, Mommy. It was like a club-restaurant. It stayed open late."

"Someone let you into a club? You're fifteen. I'm gonna have that place closed down!"

I just wanted to cry. My lies were making this worse and worse. I wasn't going to say another word. If my mother asked me anything else, I was going to plead the Fifth—just like I saw those people do on *Law and Order*. It worked for them, and I prayed it would work with the judge.

But it didn't look like my mother had any more questions. She closed her eyes and held her head, as if I'd given her some kind of headache. I could understand it—I had a serious headache myself.

She glared at me when she opened her eyes. "Where is your cell phone?"

I handed her my Sidekick.

"Stay right here in your room. I don't want to hear a peep out of you. Stay off the computer. Stay off the other phone. Don't turn on the TV or radio."

"What am I supposed to do?"

"Don't ask me that right now, Diamond."

I didn't know what that meant, but I had a feeling that I didn't want to know.

"Why don't you try studying?" my mother said. "You haven't been doing much of that these days." She slammed the door after she stomped from my room.

Whoa! I couldn't ever remember being in this much trouble. Not even my father would be able to save me from this, and I didn't have a phone to call my brother. This was beyond bad. This was really, really bad.

It was hard being banished to my room.

Glancing at the clock, I knew that my father would be home from his golf game soon. And the judge would be waiting for him. Ready to tell him every little single thing that I'd done wrong.

I just hoped that my father would understand. The judge would never listen to me, but maybe my dad would. All I had to do was explain to him what I'd been thinking, what I was doing. And then, he'd explain it all to the judge.

I rolled off my bed and began to walk back and forth. It was hard to put my thoughts together when I didn't even know what was going on. Definitely, Jax had tried to call me—I was sure of that. But since I hadn't called him back, he probably thought that I was mad at him or something.

This was impossible. I was spending my first day as Jax's girlfriend locked away in my bedroom.

And then, there was India. If the judge had spoken to Ms. Tova, then I knew Ms. Tova had said something to India. I hoped she hadn't gotten into too much trouble because of me.

The knock on my door made me forget every thought I had about my friends. When my mother and father walked into my bedroom, the look on my dad's face told me that I had a lot of talking to do if I was going to get him on my side. But he didn't give me the chance to say anything.

"Diamond, sit down."

His voice sounded deep, sounded scary.

My father stood over me, glaring down, his arms folded. And next to him stood the judge. The two of them stared me down, and I knew there was no chance to plead my case. They had already pronounced me guilty.

"I cannot remember a time when I've been more disappointed in you," my father said.

"Daddy, please. I'm sorry I lied, but—"

"There are no buts when it comes to lying. No excuses at all."

"I just want to explain."

My father motioned for me to go ahead.

"I knew you and Mother wouldn't let me go on a date."

"We've discussed that," he said.

"But you said that I could date when I was sixteen. And I'm almost sixteen. I didn't think you'd be mad about it."

"That's another lie, Diamond, because if you didn't think we'd be upset, you would have introduced us to this boy. You would have told us that you were going out. You wouldn't have brought your friends and their families into the lie with you. Do you know how upset Tova was?"

I shook my head no, but I could imagine. That meant that India was in trouble, too. I really hated that.

My father said, "What you did was wrong." He stopped and stared, as if he expected me to agree.

But I wasn't going to do that. Not until he really listened to me.

When I didn't say anything, my father continued, "Who is this boy?"

There was no need to lie here. "Jason Xavier. He's the star of the basketball team."

My father leaned back a little as if he was thinking about what I'd said. "Xavier. I know his father, Paul. We're going to speak to his parents."

That thought made me want to die. How embarrassing! "Daddy, please, don't. I don't want to get anyone else in trouble."

"You should have thought of that before you started all of these lies."

"But Jax didn't know that you and Mother didn't want me to date. I didn't tell him. He thought it was okay with you, and he even brought me home last night."

My father nodded, as if he was thinking about what I'd said. "For starters, you're grounded."

I guess I expected that. "For how long?"

"Don't even ask us that." I'd never heard my mother growl before. It was really scary. "One thing for sure—all you'll do is go to school and then come home. And on the weekends, you'll be right here, except for church."

I frowned. That didn't make any sense. "What about dance practice? And what about the Divine Divas?"

"I guess you won't be participating in either this semester," my mother said.

"Mommy, no! Daddy, please!" I jumped off my bed. "I'm so sorry, but you can't pull me out of the Divine Divas. It's in two weeks, and India, Veronique, and Aaliyah are depending on me!"

"You should have thought of that before."

"But what will happen to the group?"

My father said, "I don't know, and frankly, your mother and I don't care about that right now. All we care about is you. And what is happening to you. Your grades, and now lying and sneaking around behind our backs. Dragging other people into your mess. Coming home in the middle of the night. Diamond, I don't know what's gotten into you."

I tried to form my thoughts and my words to convince them that I was sorry. That they couldn't do this to me. But by the time I thought of anything to say, they were gone.

I fell across my bed and cried. I had worked hard to be part of the Divine Divas. And I had worked hard to be with Jax. Now everything I had worked for was being taken away from me.

And the worst part was, it would be two days before I would be able to even talk to my boyfriend.

26

I searched through the members of the young adult choir before I spotted my crew. They were hanging in the corner of the music room with their heads bent together. Looked like they were sharing secrets—my secrets.

"Hey."

The look in their eyes let me know that I was right. I could tell that India was in the middle of telling the story—my story.

The way India glared at me scared me a little. She never got pissed at anyone. But the way she looked now, like she was about to haul off and slap me or something, had me a little worried.

"Before you say anything," I started, "I'm really sorry, India." I sat in a chair next to her. "I am so, so sorry."

"Do you know how much trouble I'm in?" India said. "Not only was my mom mad at me, but your mom was mad at me, too! I told you that I was afraid to do it, and now I'm grounded for a week because of you!"

"At least it's only a week. I'm grounded and I don't know if I'll ever get off punishment."

Aaliyah said, "Okay, back up. What's going on?"

"Didn't India tell you?"

"I was just starting to when you came in."

I sighed. "I went on a date with Jax on Friday and India covered for me."

"What?" Aaliyah said. "I thought you said you were over him."

I peeked at Veronique to see if she was going to say anything, but my girl sat there with her arms folded, like she was waiting to hear the whole story.

"I was over him," I continued. "But then we got back together and went out on Friday. To make a long story short, he wanted to stay out all night and I didn't. So, he took me home and I got caught. And since India was covering for me, she got caught, too."

"Dang!" Aaliyah said.

"So, you didn't stay with him all night?" India asked. But before I could answer, India said, "That explains it."

India stared at me, and inside, I begged her not to say it. But she started to anyway. "So, you didn't—"

Before she could say more, I said, "No!" For some reason, I didn't want my girls to know what I'd done. Yeah, we were sisters and shared everything, but this date with Jax was beyond embarrassing. I just couldn't tell them—at least not yet.

Aaliyah said, "Okay, back up again. You were going to spend the night with Jax? Don't tell me you were going to—"

"No! Absolutely not." When India frowned at me, I said, "I thought about it, but then I didn't want to. That's why I went home instead of staying with him all night."

"Wow!" Aaliyah said.

India and even Veronique seemed relieved, but I was

sad. One of the best times of my life and I couldn't share it with my crew.

"So, you're both grounded?"

India nodded, but I said, "I'm worse than grounded. My parents are taking me out of everything—I'm off the dance team, and I'm out of the Divine Divas."

"What?" all three of them yelled together.

"Yeah, but you guys should still go on. You're the best, and I know you can win."

A few moments ago, India was mad and Veronique was annoyed. Now my crew just hugged me and tried to console me with their words.

"Your parents wouldn't make you really drop out," India said.

"Yeah, my sistah, they're just trying to scare you. You know how parents are."

"And remember," Aaliyah said when it was her turn, "it was your mom who was so excited. Remember how she wanted to pay for everything? She's not going to let you miss out on this big chance. She'll come around."

I wished that their words were true, but none of them had seen my parents' faces or lived in the house with them these last twenty-four hours.

Like my dad and the judge promised, I was stuck in my room all day, without my cell phone and MP3 player, without watching television or listening to the radio. Even my computer was off limits. All I could do was study and read.

And when my mother had brought me a tuna fish sandwich and a glass of water for lunch, I hadn't believed they were even going to make me eat in my bedroom. All that had been missing was a pair of gray-striped prison pajamas.

"You'll be eating your dinner up here, too," was all the judge had said to me when she'd dropped the paper plate on my desk.

Dang! I'd thought then, and I was thinking the same thing now. This was some mad mess. There was nothing my crew or anyone could do to fix it.

I shook my head to let my girls know that there was no hope. "It's not just the judge who's mad. My dad was as mad as my mother. And you know if I can't get him on my side, then I don't have any chance of changing my mother's mind." I sighed. "No matter what, it's over for me and the divas." I stopped for a second. "But I want you guys to go on." I really wanted to convince them. "You're going to win; I can feel it. And I'll be your biggest fan."

"How are we going to do this without you?" Veronique asked. "I don't want to."

"Me neither," India added. "This was your idea, and it wouldn't be fair for us to sing now."

Aaliyah said, "Maybe if we tell your mom and dad that either we do this together or we don't do it at all, they'll listen."

This was why they were my girls. We might fuss and fight and get on each other's nerves, but when it all came down, my girls had my back all . . . the . . . time. But their determination was not going to help here.

"I'm telling you, it's over. My dad and the judge won't talk to you guys; they're barely talking to me."

"Yeah," India said. "And they certainly won't listen to a word I have to say."

I said, "They're so mad right now, they wouldn't listen to Pastor Ford. I don't even think God could come down from heaven and make them change their minds. But thanks for having my back like this."

"That's just the way we do, my sistah."

"You guys are the best, but please go on. Do this for me. I don't want to stop your dreams."

"Well, you know this ain't my dream," Aaliyah said.

"Mine neither," India said.

Before Veronique could say anything, Jackie shouted for us to line up to march into the sanctuary. We stood and my crew hugged me, letting me know that no matter what, it was all going to be all right.

As I walked behind Veronique, I really hoped that my girls would go on with the Divine Divas. I was sick that I wasn't going to be with them, but I knew that this had become their dream, too, no matter what they said.

We sat in the choir stand and I couldn't help but glance at my parents, who sat just a few rows away from us. Like always, they looked back at me. But today, they didn't smile the way I was used to. Instead, they just stared as if they didn't even know me.

Well, they *didn't* know me. I was different. I was a woman now. But it was weird, because I was a woman on punishment. And I was a woman who had to keep this a secret.

There was only one person I could depend on now. Jax. I hadn't spoken to him since he'd dropped me off at home. I wished I could somehow sneak a peek at my cell. See how many times he'd tried to call me. At least we'd get to spend some time in school together now. Since he was my boyfriend, he wouldn't be keeping our relationship on the down low anymore.

I'd have to tell my girls that Jax and I were a couple. But

I wasn't worried about that. They might be pissed at first, but once they saw us together, they'd know it was for real this time.

Still, this was a tough, tough way to start a relationship. Being grounded, not having phone privileges, keeping secrets. But tomorrow I'd explain everything to Jax. And just like how he helped me with my parents and my biology test, he'd help me figure this out, too. He'd figure out what to do, and I knew he would do everything he could to make sure that we could be together.

I was counting the minutes until I would see Jax tomorrow.

27

I couldn't wait to see my boyfriend.

I hung out near his locker, but when the first-period bell rang, I had to rush to my class. I couldn't afford to be late, couldn't afford to have any kind of bad reports getting back to my parents.

In the cafeteria during lunch, I sat at the end of the table so that Jax would see me the moment he came in there. As I pretended to listen to my girls debate about whether they were going to continue with the Divine Divas, my eyes stayed on the door so that I would see my boyfriend as soon as he walked in.

"So, is that okay with you, Diamond?" India asked.

"Huh?"

"We're going to keep on with the Divine Divas," Veronique said.

"That's good." I wanted to say more, really wanted to encourage them, because I was happy for my girls. I wanted them to keep on singing, to go out there and win that contest. I would have told them all of that if Jax hadn't been so heavy on my mind.

By the end of the day, I was going crazy. Where was he?

Now that we were a couple, I thought he would have been looking for me.

I gathered my books from my locker and glanced at my watch. An hour—that was all the time I had to get home before the judge would be calling to make sure I was there.

"Be home by quarter to four," my mother had demanded this morning. The warning in her voice had left me no room to argue. It was official—I was on serious lockdown.

But I couldn't go home without seeing Jax, even if it was only for a few minutes. I was sure he'd be in the gym—at practice. As I rushed there, I planned it all in my mind—how I'd talk quickly, explain everything. And then Jax would come up with a plan, some way that we could talk tonight. Maybe I could sneak and use the phone in the kitchen after my parents went to bed.

I peeked into the gym. I was right—there was Jax. Finally! I was so happy to see him. Until I realized that he wasn't alone. I stared through the small window in the door and saw what I didn't want to see. Jax. With Jayde. Sitting on the bleachers together. He was holding her hand the way he was supposed to be holding mine. And then he kissed her. The way he was supposed to be kissing me.

It was disgusting to watch, but I couldn't turn away. Jayde was kissing my boyfriend! What was I supposed to do? What I wanted to do was run into that gym and kick her butt. But did I really want to get into a fight at school? Holy Cross Prep had a zero-tolerance policy when it came to fighting. The principal, Ms. Williams, told us over and over that we would be suspended for a week if we were ever found fighting on school premises. And with what I was going through at home, I didn't need that right now. So all I could do was brush away the tears that kept rolling out of my eyes.

It took a lot for me to finally turn away and go into the bathroom. I had to wash my face; I didn't want anyone to see me crying like this.

"Oh, God." I leaned against the sink and tried to hold my tears back, but they just wouldn't stop.

The bathroom door swung open and Jayde walked in. I was shocked, but not too shocked to turn on the water and lower my face into the sink.

"Hey, Diamond."

I pretended that I couldn't talk with all the water on my face.

But that didn't stop Jayde from going on. "I'm glad I ran into you. I just heard that you were dropping off the dance team. What's up with that?"

I grabbed a paper towel and covered my face. But I still didn't look at her. "I had to make a choice between the dance team and the Divine Divas."

"I heard about your group. Word is you guys are good. You think you might win?"

Now I turned to her. And I couldn't stop staring at her lips. "I don't know if we'll win or not. But everyone is making plans for us to be in this contest for a long time. So I don't have time for something little like the dance squad."

"I guess." Jayde grinned. "We're just small stuff to you now, huh?"

I wanted to forget all about that suspension rule for fighting. I just wanted to beat her down right there on the bathroom floor. "Yeah, *you're* small stuff."

"Well, no biggie. The dance team will go on without

you. See ya." She waved and smiled as if she was so happy. I guess she was, since she was trying to steal my boyfriend.

I needed to talk to Jax, but when I looked at my watch again, my time had run out. If I wasn't home in thirty minutes, I might be grounded until I was fifty. I couldn't take any more chances. Jax would have to wait. But when I did catch up with him, he was going to have some serious explaining to do. Serious explaining before I would even consider taking him back.

$\mathcal{M}$s. Winters?" Mr. Berg called my name as if he was surprised I was raising my hand. "You know the answer?"

"Yes," I said with an attitude. "That's a parallelogram. The opposite sides are parallel and congruent."

"Very good, Ms. Winters."

Of course it was good. For the last five days all I'd been doing in school was shocking my teachers. It wasn't like I had anything else to do. I'd been on lockdown since Saturday—a week of doing nothing except studying. For the first time in my life, I was thrilled to come to school. At least I saw people, saw my girls. I got out of that prison.

Every day, my mother called home at exactly three-forty-five. And then, she was home before five—before Carmen even left. It was like she had grounded herself just to make me more miserable.

When the bell rang for the end of the period, I took my time gathering my math books. I wasn't in any rush to get to the cafeteria. I was hoping to run into Jax in the halls somewhere, hoping today would be the day he wouldn't ignore me, the way he'd been doing all week—ever since I saw him with Jayde on Monday.

Yesterday, I had even gotten the nerve to call out to him

when he'd passed by, but he'd kept on walking. Hadn't even bothered to look at me. Just kept moving as if he'd never known me.

"Hey!" Aaliyah came up behind me. "Why're you walking so slow?"

"No reason."

"Come on; let's get to the cafeteria so that we can beat the line."

Inside the lunchroom, Veronique was already at our table, eating a sandwich that she'd brought from home. She said, "India's waiting for you," and she pointed to India, who was already standing in line.

But the moment we got to India, the cafeteria exploded with applause. I turned and saw Jax and the rest of the basketball team strolling in. Of course, Jax bounced his ball down the center of the room.

"I heard they had another big win last night," India said. "So they're undefeated."

"Good for the team, but I can't stand that boy," Aaliyah said, like she did every time she saw Jax.

"Me neither."

This was the first time I'd ever heard India say a bad word about anyone. Both of them looked at me as if they were waiting for me to agree, but I didn't say anything. I was just so, so glad that I hadn't told any of my crew that I'd had sex with him. Especially now that he was pretending that he'd never even known my name.

"So, what do you think about Jax?" Aaliyah pushed it.

I shrugged my shoulders, like seeing him was no big deal. "I didn't have a good time on that date anyway. And all the trouble I got in? It was not worth it. I am so over him."

"Really?" Aaliyah sounded like she didn't believe me. Like she'd heard that line before.

"Definitely," I said as strongly as I could. "And I mean it this time."

But inside, I couldn't believe the way I hurt. A week ago today, I'd had sex for the first time, and what should have been the happiest time of my life was the worst. I was stuck at home doing nothing but homework. And I'd lost my boyfriend before we'd even gotten started.

I watched Jax stroll around the cafeteria, pointing at guys, hugging all the girls. Even when I passed by his table with my tray, he ignored me. How could he do this after we'd made love?

I remembered the way he'd kissed me. Like he'd loved me. I remembered all the words he'd said. Like he'd cared for me more than anyone he'd ever known. This couldn't be about him not wanting me anymore. There had to be something that I was missing.

I could barely eat my hamburger as I watched Jax kissing on every girl that stepped to him. And every time he kissed one of them, I wondered, What happened to us?

Maybe he had gotten into trouble. Maybe my parents had called his parents. Or maybe he was mad because he'd been calling me and I hadn't returned his calls.

That was it!

I hadn't thought about it before, but Jax had probably been calling and calling me. When I hadn't answered my cell, he'd thought that I was mad at him. Must have thought that I was ignoring him. All this time I'd been thinking he didn't want to have anything to do with me, but he had to have been thinking that I didn't want to have anything to do with him.

As Jax walked toward the exit, I pushed my tray aside. "I've gotta go," I said to my crew.

"What's up?" Aaliyah asked.

"Nothing. I'm just trying to make up some extra credit in English. I'll catch you guys later."

I dumped my tray on the rack and ran after Jax. But in the hall, I didn't see him. And then he appeared. Walked right out of the restroom and stopped in front of me.

"Hey, Jax," I said.

He had the nerve to point his finger at me. Like I was just one of the regular girls in school. "What's up?"

"Can I talk to you?"

"Talk." He began bouncing his basketball.

Everyone was starting to come out of the cafeteria and I didn't want anyone to hear us. And I especially didn't want my girls to see us.

"This is private."

He shrugged. "I got five minutes. Let's duck in here."

I followed him into the gym, and he bounced that ball as if I wasn't there. I stood to the side as he raced up, then down, the court. Made a few baskets. Then finally he came over to me as if he'd just remembered that I was there.

"What's up?" he asked.

With my arms folded, I asked, "I wanted to know what happened? Why are you ignoring me?"

"I'm not ignoring you."

"That's the way it seems to me."

"You're wrong, babe." He bounced the ball between his legs, back and forth, like he was doing some kind of drill.

Well, at least he'd called me babe. That was a good sign. "Okay." I waited for Jax to say something else. Something like he'd been missing me since we hadn't said a word to

each other in a week. Or how great a time he'd had with me
at the hotel.

But he didn't say another word. Just kept bouncing that
basketball.

I wasn't sure what I was supposed to say. It was good to
know that he wasn't mad and that we were still a couple.
But I still needed to know the deal about why he'd been
kissing Jayde. That was not cool and he needed to know
that.

I said, "I haven't been able to call you because my parents took my cell phone away from me last week."

He shrugged. "No sweat."

I frowned. "Well, I know you've been calling. And since
we're a couple now, I wanted to explain—"

"Whoa, hold up." The ball bouncing stopped. "A couple? Who said we were a couple?"

"You said—"

"No, I didn't."

"But . . . but I thought since we made love."

"Oh, hey." He held up his hands like he was under arrest and started backing away from me. "Look, we were just
kicking it."

"Kicking it?" I wasn't even sure what that meant. "I
wasn't kicking anything."

"Yeah, you were. We were both just kicking it. It was
nothing special."

"Nothing special?" I screamed, then lowered my voice.
"It was special to me."

"Sorry 'bout that. I just thought you wanted to have a
little fun."

"How could you think that? I never said that. I didn't
even want to do it."

"Ah, come on. You wanted to do it. No one does anything they don't want to do."

I was trying so hard not to cry. But Jax was making that almost impossible. "What about all those things you said to me?"

"What about them?"

"You said you really cared about me."

"Well, I did."

Did? "You said that we were in love."

"Yeah, that's what I thought. But then I got back with my girlfriend."

Girlfriend? Now, I know I always thought I was having a heart attack, but I was sure that it was for real this time. My heart was pounding so hard, it felt like it was going to come right through my chest. "I didn't know you had a girlfriend," I said, trying to keep the tears away, trying to stay cool. "Why didn't you tell me that?"

"You never asked." He was much cooler than I was. "Hey, I gotta make this run. Holla."

And then he left. Just left me standing there. Like he barely knew me. Like we had never had sex together.

I staggered over to the bleachers. I couldn't wrap my brain around everything that Jax had just said. We were just kicking it, those were his words. But that's not what had happened. I wouldn't just kick it with a boy that way.

There were so many words running around in my head. I remembered all the things Jax had said to me before. And then what he'd said today. I tried to put them together, but they didn't add up. Nothing he'd said—not before and not today—made any sense any more.

But after a few minutes, it became clear. What Jax had said today was the truth. What he'd said on all those other days had been a lie. It was all just so I'd have sex with him.

It had been a game. And now the game was over. He'd won. I'd lost.

Even when the bell rang for next period, I didn't move. I couldn't. All I could do was sit and think about what I'd done. What I had given up. And for what? Jax didn't even want to know me now.

For the last week, I'd thought I'd been living the worst days of my life. But I'd been wrong. Big time!

No day would ever be worse than today.

29

The moment I walked into my house, I cried.

I leaned against the front door and just let it all out—all of the tears that I'd been holding since Jax had left me sitting in that gym. It had been hard not to let anyone see what I was feeling, but I'd kept it all in through my last two classes. And then after school, I'd dashed out of that place, not even stopping by my locker to connect with my crew. I couldn't let them see me like this. One look and my girls would know something was up. Even though Aaliyah always gave me grief, she would have been the first to notice, the first to care, the first to get the truth out of me. I was too embarrassed to let them know what I'd done. And even more embarrassed to let them know that Jax had just basically kicked me to the curb.

I was so glad to be home, where I could cry in peace. Where no one would see me. No one would hear me. I wished so badly that I could tell someone about this—but I never could. And just the thought of having to handle this all alone made me hurt even more.

"Diamond?"

I was shocked to hear her voice. Carmen was always off on Fridays. Why did she have to be here today?

"Diamond?"

And then I saw her. It wasn't Carmen. It was my mother.

I tried to wipe my tears away, but I wasn't fast enough. And I wasn't strong enough. I was still crying when she rushed down the hall to me.

"What's wrong, sweetheart?"

Her look of horror was worse than any mother-eye that she'd ever given me. There was no suspicion or mistrust on her face. All I could see was her love, and that made me cry more.

She wrapped her arms around me. "Diamond, please, tell me what's wrong?"

With everything inside of me, I wanted to tell her all about Jax—what we'd done, what he'd done. But I couldn't. The judge would kill me, and as bad as I felt, I wasn't ready to die.

The moment my mother let go of me, I dropped my bag and ran up the stairs. Inside my bedroom, I slammed the door and crashed onto my bed.

But it wasn't like that was enough to stop the judge. She was right behind me.

I buried my face in my pillows, but my mother wasn't having it. She pulled me into her arms. "Tell me what's wrong."

All I could do was cry.

She just held me. And I just cried, until she asked, "Is this about the Divine Divas?"

That seemed as good an excuse as anything. So I nodded.

"Sweetheart, I know you're upset about that, but your father and I were going to talk to you tonight."

I sobbed some more.

She said, "There's no reason to cry." She used the tips of her fingers to wipe the tears from my face. "Your father and I talked. And we talked to Pastor Ford. Although we're still very much upset with what you did, I guess we've been able to calm down a little. And we think you're on your way to learning your lesson."

Learning my lesson? My mother had no idea!

"Sweetheart, listen to me. We're letting you continue with the group. You can be a part of the Divine Divas."

"Really?" I sniffed.

"Yes. You worked hard with the divas. All of you girls have. So we're letting up on that part of your punishment. I'm still holding off on the dance team. I think doing all of that was too much for you."

"It was."

My mother gave me a tiny smile. "Diamond Winters, are you agreeing with me?"

I nodded. "Thank you for letting me be part of the Divine Divas again."

Her arms were still around me when she said, "You're welcome. Now, we're still going to hold your phone and hold off on your other privileges for a couple of more weeks."

"That's okay." My voice still quivered a little.

"That's okay? Wow, I guess you are growing up."

"I'm trying to, Mommy. I really am."

"I know you are, sweetheart. The thing is, we want to be able to trust you, Diamond. When your father and I are not around, we have to know that you'll do the right thing. You understand that, don't you?"

She was making this so hard for me—my guilt was just

growing, because if she ever found out what I'd done with Jax, my mother would never trust me again. But I nodded anyway. "Yes, Mommy."

Her lecture continued, "There are always consequences for sneaking and lying and cheating, Diamond. There's always a price to pay."

She had no idea how much I was *really* suffering from the consequences. I wanted her to stop talking, but I didn't want her to stop holding me. So I just laid my head on her shoulder and listened.

She said, "We're giving you another chance, but people don't always get a second chance. Remember that, sweetheart."

I was getting a second chance with the Divine Divas; I was really happy about that. But I'd never get another chance to be a virgin. I don't know why, but suddenly that seemed real important. Seemed like something special was gone from me forever. Made me want to start crying all over again.

My mother let me stay with my head resting on her, and I wished that I could stay right there forever. When my mother asked, "Are you feeling better?" I almost wanted to tell her no just so she'd keep holding me.

"Yes." I hugged her. "Thanks, Mommy. Thank you for giving me another chance. I promise, I'm going to be perfect from now on."

My mother laughed just a little. "We don't want you to be perfect, dear. No one is perfect. We just want you to try your best. And to understand integrity. Your word is so important; what you say and what you do is who you are. And your father and I want you to be the best that you can be."

"I'm going to try."

"Trying is all we ask. You're going to make mistakes; we all do, but just be honest. If you tell the truth, I think you'll be surprised the way things will work out for you." My mother looked me in my eyes. "Telling the truth isn't always easy, but I want you to know there will never be anything that you tell me that will make me stop loving you. You are my daughter, my Diamond. I gave you that name because you are so precious to me. And I will love you always. Okay."

I nodded.

My mother kissed my forehead and walked to the door. But suddenly, she turned around. Gave me that look again, that mother-eye that let me know she knew something. "Are you sure everything is all right, sweetheart?"

Inside, I screamed no over and over. I wanted so bad to tell her that my head hurt and my heart hurt and that Jax had made it all hurt. But I was too scared. She said she would always love me, but she didn't know what I'd done. Having sex with Jax might be the one thing that could make her not love me anymore.

"I'm okay, Mommy." And then I tried to smile so that she would believe me.

The way she still stared let me know that there was more on her mind. "Just remember," she said. "You can talk to me about anything."

I felt like I was going to burst inside. "Everything is all right, Mommy."

For the first time since I came home, my mother really smiled. I felt bad, but at least my lie helped my mother feel good. I'd done the right thing.

"Your father will be home late tonight, so I thought we'd just order in a pizza. What do you think?"

"Okay."

"With pineapple?"

Now I knew this was all about my mother making me feel better. She would *never* eat pineapples on *her* pizza.

"I love you, sweetheart," she said before she walked into the hallway. As soon as she left me, the ache in my heart got worse.

I lay down on my bed, closed my eyes, and cried some more. How was I supposed to handle this all by myself?

I had never felt so alone. All alone.

I was still crying, even though I tried to keep it quiet. I didn't want my mother to hear me, because then she would know that I wasn't crying about the Divine Divas. But every time I tried to stop, I'd think about Jax. I'd think about what we'd done. And then I'd think about all of the horrible stuff he'd said.

I couldn't take it anymore.

I jumped up. "Mommy!"

She rushed from her office, two rooms away from my bedroom. "What's wrong, sweetheart?"

My plan had been to tell her, but now when I looked at her, I didn't have the right words. I was scared. She wouldn't love me anymore. There was no way she could after what I'd done.

I cried and she took my hand. I followed her into her bedroom and sat next to her on my parents' king-sized bed. She held me some more, and I wondered how many tears God put inside of you. At this rate, I might cry all night.

"Mommy, I have something to tell you."

"Okay."

I opened my mouth, but no words would come out.

"Diamond, you can tell me anything. I told you that."

"But suppose—"

She didn't let me finish. "Suppose nothing." Then she made it easier for me. She leaned back against the huge pillows on her bed, and she laid my head on her chest. "When you're ready, just begin," she said.

I don't know if it took me seconds or minutes. But I took a deep breath. "Mommy, when Jax and I went out . . . he took me to a hotel. . . ."

I wanted to stop right there, but my mother held me tighter and I kept going.

"And then . . . we had . . . sex." I held my breath, closed my eyes tight, and waited for her to freak out. I waited for her to throw me off the bed and demand that I go to my room forever.

But she didn't push me away. Or yell at me. All she did was hold me tighter. I wondered if she'd even heard me. But there was no way I was going to repeat what I'd just said.

I said, "Mom, I only did it because I really thought that he loved me."

"I know, sweetheart."

It was the way she said it—like *she* still loved me—that made me keep talking. I told her everything—how Jax had called me every night, how he'd said such wonderful things, how he'd convinced me to go to the hotel, and finally, what he'd told me today.

"He acted like he didn't even know me, Mommy. Why did he do that?" Just the thought of that made me want to cry all over again, but I was too tired to do that anymore.

"I don't know, baby."

"He was so mean, and now I know that he didn't care about me at all. He just wanted to have sex."

"Sometimes it seems like sex is the only thing on young people's minds."

"It wasn't on my mind, Mom. I really wanted to stay a virgin. But after Jax started talking to me, it didn't seem like being a virgin was so important anymore. Especially since I thought that maybe one day I would marry Jax."

Now that I said that out loud, it really sounded dumb. "I guess you think that was pretty stupid."

"No, sweetheart." She hugged me tighter. "That wasn't stupid. It was the way you felt. The way Jax made you feel."

I couldn't believe I was sitting on the bed with my mother talking like this. She'd punished me for things like talking on the phone for too long or too late. Or for getting an attitude with her when she asked me to do something. Or for many other things—nothing that was nearly as big as what I'd just told her.

But this time, it didn't seem like she was mad at me at all. She just held me and talked to me. I knew the punishment could still be coming, but that didn't matter right now. All I wanted to do was to stay like this, right here with my mother.

I just kept on talking. "When I met Jax, I thought he was really cool, really nice. But he fooled me. He's a jerk. I don't think there's a worse person on the earth than him."

"Well, I don't know Jax, but even with all of this, I can't say that he's a bad person."

That surprised me. I thought my mother would be ready to hit the streets looking for Jax. Ready to have him thrown in jail or something. "I thought you'd be mad at him. I thought you'd be mad at me."

"I'm not mad. I'm upset. I'm disappointed. And I'm worried about you." She sighed as if there was a lot on her mind. "I'm so sorry, baby."

That made me sit up and look right at her. "You're sorry? Mom, I'm sorry. I know I disappointed you, and I never wanted to do that."

"I know you didn't, but I let you down, too." My mother looked at me as if this was the first time she was seeing me. And her eyes were wet, like now she wanted to cry. "I let you down because you and I should have talked about this a long time ago."

"But how could we? You didn't know this was going to happen. You didn't know Jax was going to do this."

"Yes, I did, sweetheart. You've never been my age, but I've been yours. I know the things that teenagers go through. I didn't know it would be Jax, and I didn't know that it would happen now. But I knew that sooner or later some boy would step to you this way. It's just the way the world is, and I should have prepared you."

Now I really felt awful. This was my fault, but what I'd done had my mother feeling bad. "Mommy, this wasn't you. I knew I shouldn't have done it. I know what you and Daddy and Pastor Ford have been telling me. Even Vee tried to tell me—"

"You talked to Veronique about this?"

"Uh-huh. I told her what Jax wanted me to do and she told me not to do it."

My mother sounded really sad when she said, "I wish you had come to me."

I didn't know what to say, until she hugged me again. "I'll come to you next time. I promise, Mommy."

"I hope so, sweetheart. I want you to feel like you can talk to me about anything."

"I'm just always so worried about getting in trouble."

"Well, maybe your dad and I need to do something about that. You're a young woman now, and we have to find a way to make sure that you can come to us no matter what. Maybe we need to look at some of the rules around here, if that will help."

Was my mother kidding me? I'd just told her that I'd had sex with a boy who'd kicked me to the curb and she was talking about listening to me. If I believed in aliens, I would have sworn that one had come and taken my real mother away.

"Now, I'm not saying we're changing anything yet," my mother said. "And the rest of your punishment still stands. But we'll talk. Your father, you, and I will sit down. And we'll talk."

I was feeling so bad about Jax, but so good about my mother. If I had known she was going to act like this, I would have talked to her a long time ago. And then maybe this whole thing with Jax wouldn't have happened.

"Thank you, Mom. Thank you for not being mad."

"This is not something for me to be mad about. I'm sad that you didn't come to me before, but I'm so glad that you came to me now."

"So am I."

"Are you all right?"

I shrugged. "I still feel bad. Really, really bad. And I feel guilty. And a little stupid."

"You're not stupid. You know that, right?"

"I guess. But why did I do that with Jax?"

"You trusted him. But what I want is for you to learn to trust yourself. Never let anyone talk you into something that you really don't want to do."

"I want to learn how to do that."

"Well then, we'll just have to talk more often. You and I. On the regular."

I grinned. There my mom went again. Trying to sound hip. But this time, she didn't sound so old.

My mom said, "We'll work out something. Put it on our calendars. Maybe once a week. Go shopping, go to the movies. But the most important thing is we'll talk. Just you and me."

"That would be great, Mom." I hugged her. "You're the absolute best."

"I am, huh? Well, go change your clothes. I was going to order a pizza, but I think we need to go out."

I jumped from the bed. "Mom, can we? That would be awesome. I've been stuck in this house like . . ." I stopped. My mother was being nice, but I didn't want to push it too much. I asked, "Can we go to Friday's?"

My mother rolled her eyes, but this time I knew she was just kidding. "Don't you know there are other restaurants besides Friday's? Okay," she said, as if she was giving in. But I knew she was fine with going there.

"I'll be ready in five minutes," I said.

Before I left her bedroom, my mother's serious voice came back. "There is one thing, Diamond. I'm going to make an appointment for you to see a doctor."

I frowned. "Why?"

"I just want to make sure that you're okay."

"But I am okay."

"I'm sure you are. But I'm your mother. And I want it verified for myself, okay?"

My mother had almost made me feel good about everything that had happened. If this would make her happy, then I would just do it. "Okay."

"And anyway," she said, "I'm the *judge*. And the *judge* has spoken."

The way my mother said that and the way she smiled, I wondered if she knew that was my nickname for her. But today, she wasn't close to being the judge.

Today, she just felt like Mommy.

30

This was so weird.

I'd just told my mom the biggest secret of my life and here we were hanging at Friday's. It almost felt like none of that stuff I told her about Jax mattered. Even though I could tell that it did matter, because sometimes while I was talking, my mom would get this look in her eyes like she was really sad. But then right away, she would be happy again and would start talking and laughing with me.

The best part was that my mother hadn't said a word about Jax, and what was even better was that she hadn't said anything about school. All she wanted to do was talk about everything that I loved—especially fashion.

"I get all of my ideas from my magazines," I told her.

"I have to admit, you have quite a knack for it."

I stood up and twirled like I was a model, showing off my short swingy skirt with the blue plaid flats I was wearing. And I felt really good when I sat back down and my mom was laughing.

"Well maybe you and I should take a long weekend trip and do some shopping in London or Paris."

"Really? Oh, Mom, that would be great!"

All I could think about as I sucked on my Jack Daniels

ribs was how being with my mom was so cool. Just a little while ago, I'd been so scared to tell her about Jax. I was sure that I was going to be in some serious trouble. But it was like telling the truth freed me in some way. My mom always said that I would never be punished for telling the truth—only for lying, and sneaking, and cheating. I guess this proved that she was right.

Telling the truth had opened up a whole new door for us. Like once I was honest with her, she could listen to me. For the first time, I felt like she wanted to really know who I was.

This was the best time I'd ever had in my life with my mom. She was really trying to make me forget about Jax. My happy was almost back.

But then, we went home.

The moment my mother turned into the driveway and I saw my dad's Navigator, I was scared all over again.

"Mom," I said when she opened the car door to get out. "Can we . . ." I closed my eyes and said a quick prayer. Things had been going so well, I just hoped that my mother would do this one last thing for me. "Can we just keep this between you and me? I don't want to tell Daddy."

My mom sighed and then took my hand. "Diamond, I don't keep secrets from your father." Her voice was soft, but it was strong, like she wasn't going to change her mind.

"But it's not your secret. It's mine."

"No. It belongs to both of us now and it shouldn't stay a secret. Your father needs to know." When I still didn't move, my mother said, "You know, if you don't tell your father, you'll be lying to him."

I shook my head. I had learned my lesson about lying— I wasn't going to do that again. That's not what I was talking about. "No, Mom. I don't want to lie; I just don't want to say anything."

"That's still lying, sweetheart. That's a lie of omission."

Okay, I had never heard that before. You could lie by not saying anything at all? That didn't make much sense to me.

My mom said, "Not telling your father is hiding something important, something that he should know. And that's lying."

My mother's words didn't do a thing to make me want to get out of that car. Telling my mother had been hard, but now I had to face my dad? There was no way I could do that. My daddy thought I was the perfect daughter and I wanted to stay that way. If I told him what I did with Jax . . . I squeezed my eyes shut. I couldn't even think about it.

Slowly, my mother got out of the car, closed her door, and then turned to me. I was still sitting, right where she left me. Then she gave me one of her mother-eyes. But this time, it wasn't the "I don't trust you, what are you up to" looks. In her eyes, I saw nothing but love. She was trying to tell me that I could do this. And that we would do it together.

So, I sucked it up, got out of the car, and walked to the front door as if I wasn't having a heart attack.

If I was lucky, my father would already be in bed.

But when we stepped into the house, my father met us right at the door. "There're my girls."

Of course he wouldn't be in bed. It wasn't even nine o'clock.

He kissed my mother, then hugged me. "Where've you been? Don't tell me you went out and had a good time without me?" He walked into the living room and when he leaned back on the couch, he laughed. But I knew he wouldn't be in a good mood much longer.

"Diamond and I went out to dinner. We had some things to talk about." My mom looked at me like it was my turn.

But I was shaking too much to say a word.

My mom said, "Diamond, do you have something to tell your father?"

I tried to look at my dad, but the way he was frowning made me just turn away. I started counting. By the time I got to five, I promised myself that I would begin talking. But no matter how hard I tried, I couldn't get past three. So I started counting all over again. One, two, three . . . and then I stopped.

I couldn't do it.

When I looked at my dad, I was crying.

"Diamond?" My dad put down his pipe and started to get up from the couch.

"Diamond?" This time, it was my mother calling me.

My father took one step toward me, and I turned to the stairs and dashed up them faster than I ever had before. I ran into my bedroom, closed the door, and then leaned against it—as if that was going to keep my parents out. This was so stupid. It wasn't like I could hide out in here. I was still in the house. I would still have to face my father.

It had been a long time since I'd thought about running away, and I was beginning to think that might not be such a bad idea now. But it didn't take me a minute to think about how dumb that was. Sure, when I was seven I thought running away would be easy. But I was grown up now—I knew running away took money. And I didn't have any!

So I just waited, and when my parents weren't right behind me, I figured my mother was probably telling my father what had happened. Once he heard everything, my dad was going to come stomping into my room, screaming that I was the worst daughter in the world and that I was grounded until I was fifty.

Maybe he would be so ashamed of me that he would send me away to live with my grandparents in Dallas. Or worse, to live with my other grandmother in Oklahoma.

That would be horrible!

I lay on my bed and waited. And waited.

I just waited for my father to come in and tell me that my whole life was over.

I didn't turn on my TV or plug in my MP3 player or do anything. All I did was lie on my bed and watch the clock. Only ten minutes had passed, but I felt like I'd been waiting for ten days.

And then, I heard their footsteps. I closed my eyes; I wanted to pray and ask God to help me wiggle out of this. But I didn't know what to say to Him.

There was one soft knock on the door before my parents walked right in.

I stayed on my bed with my eyes squeezed tight, hoping that if my daddy thought that I was asleep, he would leave and wait until tomorrow to talk to me. At least that would give me some time to figure out my strategy.

"Diamond?"

When he called my name twice, I knew the gig was up. I opened my eyes and peeked at him. My mother stood right by his side. The serious, tight look on their faces told me that I was right—my mother had told him. And the way he was pushing his lips together, I knew she'd told him everything!

He sat down on the bed next to me, but he didn't say a word. The quiet got so loud that I finally had to say something.

"Daddy, I'm sorry." I knew that sounded lame, but what else was I supposed to say?

He nodded, but it still took him a little while to figure out what he wanted to say. Finally, "I know you're sorry, sweetheart. . . ."

Okay, he was still calling me sweetheart instead of the million other names I could think of. That had to be a good sign.

"But even though you're sorry, there are some things we need to talk about."

I took a breath and sat up straight. I kept telling my parents that I was mature, so I was going to take this like a woman.

My daddy took my hand. "Your mother told me how Jason had been calling you. And how you hid everything from us."

"Because I knew you wouldn't approve," I said softly.

He nodded. "We wouldn't have. But here's the thing, Diamond. Any relationship that makes you lie to your Heavenly Father or your earthly father is not a relationship worth having."

Okay, my dad needed to stop right there because this couldn't get any worse. Not only did his words make me feel bad, but it was the way he was talking. Like he had never been so disappointed in his whole life. And he was bringing God into this, too? I felt like I had let everyone in the whole world and all of heaven down.

He kept on talking, "Anything that you have to do in secret can't be good. God tells you that He doesn't want anything to be done in the dark."

I thought about all the times I talked to Jax in my closet.

"And God warns that anything done in the dark will come to light."

Ain't that the truth was what I wanted to say. But I just sat there and listened.

"I'm very disappointed in you, Diamond."

Oh, God. I already knew he was, but it was worse to hear him say it out loud. I wanted to cry all over again.

"But the key to life is taking every situation and learning something from it."

"I've learned a lot, Daddy. I'll never do anything like this again. I promise."

"It's good that you're making this promise to me, but it's more important to make it to yourself. Because while lying is always a sin, it is a tragedy when you lie to yourself."

At first, that seemed to be a little over my head. But then I thought about all the times I *had* lied to myself. I believed the things Jax was saying because I wanted to. I just wanted to think Jax was my boyfriend even though he never treated me that way. Deep inside, I knew Jax didn't really love me. So I guess that's what my dad was talking about. I had lied to myself about Jax the whole time.

But when my father said, "We're going to talk to Jason's parents," I stopped thinking about myself.

"Daddy, no!" I didn't even realized I screamed until my father gave me one of those looks that usually came only from my mother. I wasn't trying to be disrespectful or anything, but what happened with Jax had been embarrassing enough. If my father went to his parents, it would be beyond humiliating. "Daddy, I don't want to get Jax in trouble."

"I don't care if he gets in trouble or not." My father sounded like he had a major attitude. "His parents need to know what's going on. Especially since what Jason did was against the law."

Now, I knew what Jax and I had done was a sin, but how was having sex against the law? That's just what I asked my father.

"You're a minor. You're under age. He could go to jail for having sex with you."

Oh my gosh! "But Jax is a minor, too."

"I don't know all of the legal ramifications the way your mother does." My father stopped, but my mother motioned for him to continue. "And while it's rare, in California, Jax could be arrested. What he did was illegal—even if he is a minor. Not even a minor can have sex with another minor. This is serious."

I could not believe this was happening. Jax was a jerk, but I didn't want him to go to jail because of me.

"Now, your mother and I are not going to press charges."

I was so relieved about that I thought I was going to faint.

"But like I said, we are going to talk to his parents."

Well, there was nothing else for me to say. There was no hope for my saving Jax. But then, I wondered why I even wanted to save his behind? I guess it wasn't saving him that I cared about. I just didn't want the whole world to know what a dope I'd been. I didn't want everyone to know that I'd fallen for that flake so fast and so hard.

"There is something else," my father just kept on talking and I wondered if this night was ever going to end. "You have to take some responsibility for what happened with you and Jason."

I couldn't imagine what else my mother and father could do to me, but I was ready. I was going to take my punishment.

"It's getting late. We'll talk tomorrow." My father kissed me on the forehead, but it didn't feel the same way it did those millions of other times he kissed me. This time, it felt like he kissed me because he was supposed to, not because he wanted to. I had never felt worse in my life.

"Good night, dear," my mother said before she and my father left me alone.

I lay back on the bed exhausted. I hadn't said much, but listening had totally drained me.

Being fifteen was really, really hard.

31

This was worse than being on punishment.

It was bad enough that I'd hardly slept last night dreaming about what my father had said. It killed me that I had disappointed him, and in my dream I made a promise that I would never disappoint him or my mom ever again.

But now, here was my mother telling me even more bad news.

The conversation had started out good when my mom woke me up to tell me about the Divine Divas rehearsal.

"You have to get up. India, Veronique, and Aaliyah are rehearsing today."

"On Saturday?"

"Yes, the outfits came in yesterday and the girls are going to be practicing in them. Didn't they tell you?"

"No, they haven't mentioned the Divine Divas all week except to tell me that they were going to do it. I think they don't want to hurt my feelings."

"Well, you need to go to that rehearsal if you're going to be part of the group. The show's next week."

I don't know how I didn't realize it. My mom was right. The show was next week, on Wednesday. The night before Thanksgiving.

"Okay, Mom." I wasn't as happy as I thought I would be. I was glad that my mom and dad had changed their minds and they were going to let me back with my crew, but I still felt bad about what I'd done. So bad that I almost wanted to put myself on punishment.

"Thanks, Mom. Thanks for letting me be part of the Divine Divas again."

"There is a contingency to this."

That's when I knew trouble was coming. Whenever my mom used her big judge words, it was never good for me.

"Rehearsal is at two, but you have to meet with Pastor Ford first."

"Pastor Ford?" I felt another heart attack coming on.

My mother nodded. "She wants to talk to you. You have to get past her if you want to get back into the group."

"What time do we have to be there?"

My mother raised her eyebrows. "I didn't say anything about we. She wants to see you at noon."

Okay, this was going to be bad. Even on *Law & Order*, they never let children speak to the police without their parents. Suddenly, I needed my mother really bad.

"Why can't you go with me?" I was trying not to whine, but the thought of sitting with the pastor by myself was making it hard.

"This is the way Pastor Ford wants it," my mother said. "She's responsible for the people who represent our church. And if you want to rejoin the divas, you have to get past her."

"Did you tell . . ." But I stopped before I asked the whole question. I didn't have to ask; I already knew. If I was seeing the pastor, my mother and father had already told her . . . everything. Pastor Ford always said that she was our spiritual leader. And if we had challenges, then she had challenges. She was all up in everybody's business.

My plan had been to avoid my pastor for the rest of my life so that she wouldn't ever look at me. Because if she looked at me, then she would know. And I didn't want Pastor Ford to know this—what would she think of me now?

Never in a million years did I think my parents were going to tell her. This was too embarrassing. I mean, now everyone would wonder what kind of parents would have a daughter like me. I felt bad for them, because it wasn't their fault that I'd been such an idiot.

I was trying to think of a fast way to get out of this meeting, but I knew I was stuck. I'd have to face Pastor Ford if I wanted to be part of the Divine Divas. I had to talk to her whether I wanted to or not.

When my mother left me alone, I fell back on my bed and pulled the covers over my head. Being banished to my bedroom didn't seem like such a bad thing right about now.

I would rather be grounded forever than have to sit down and talk to Pastor Ford about this!

My recent track record didn't look good, but I really could wiggle my way out of just about anything. My dad was the easiest—all I had to do was smile a little, kiss him a lot, and I could have anything I wanted. My mom wasn't as easy, but except for when she was really mad, there was always a way to her heart. I just had to work a little harder to find it.

But Pastor Ford? I hadn't been in many situations like this before with my pastor. But I knew one thing; I knew that there was no wiggling around her. Pastor Ford wouldn't fall for just any old line. Part of the problem with her was that it seemed like she had a direct line to God. I'd seen it happen so many times, and it was pretty scary. Pastor Ford could look at a person and then God would tell her what was going on with them. So there wasn't a whole lotta lying going on around her. Not that I wanted to lie, but what was I supposed to say to Pastor after all the things she'd been trying to teach us in church? After all the times I'd heard her say that we should stay virgins until we were married?

"Hello, Diamond."

I was so busy worrying that I hadn't even heard Pastor come in. I was supposed to be scared, and I was, but first I had to check out Pastor's outfit. From one fashionista to another, Pastor Ford knew how to rock some clothes. That always cracked me up, since she was a pastor. And she was sort of old. But she still knew how to do it. Like this gold velour sweat suit she wore. Now this was fierce. Something I would definitely wear.

I wanted to ask her where she'd bought it, but when I followed her into her office, I remembered why I was there. And I got scared all over again.

She said, "So, I understand that we're going to have a talk today," then pointed for me to sit on the couch.

The way she said that, I wanted to tell her that this wasn't my idea. If she wanted me to go home, I would gladly do that.

"My mom said you wanted to talk to me."

"I do. I would think that you would want to talk to me, too."

No, I don't, was what I said on the inside. But on the outside, I said, "I guess."

"Good," Pastor Ford said. "Why don't you start?"

Start what? I didn't want to start a thing. It was bad enough that I had to listen, but my plan wasn't to do much talking. I just planned to take my beating and then get to the rehearsal if Pastor Ford was going to let me stay with the group.

Pastor Ford was looking at me like she expected me to say something. "Uh, I don't know where to begin," I said.

Okay, see, I was brilliant. Now Pastor Ford would have to be first. She could just start her lecture and I could just listen and get this over with.

Pastor said, "Begin at the beginning."

I guess I wasn't as smart as I thought I was. Or maybe it was just that Pastor was smarter.

"Well, I met this boy."

"Jason Xavier."

I knew my parents had told our pastor, but dang. They had named names!

"Yes."

The way my pastor looked at me, I knew that wasn't enough. Even I was getting tired of all of this stalling. So, I did what Pastor said. I began at the beginning. Told her everything. About how I'd been watching Jax ever since I got to high school. How he was the star basketball player. How he started talking to me. And then really talking to me. And finally, how I'd broken the vow to stay a virgin until I was married.

By the time I finished, I thought I'd be crying. But I wasn't. I guess I'd cried so much yesterday that there was really nothing left to cry about. It was done, over. I needed to move on.

Still, if Pastor told me that I could never sing again for

her or her church, I wouldn't have minded. I was just so tired of this drama. I wished there was a way I could begin all over again. Start my life—or at least this school year—over.

I waited for Pastor Ford to say something, but she just stayed real quiet. Like she was so mad, she couldn't even think of anything to say. I wondered if she would ever speak to me again. Wondered if she would make me and my parents and my brother leave the church for good. I kind of knew all of this stuff I was thinking was ridiculous. There were other people in the church sleeping around; I heard the grown-ups talking about it all the time. But still, I couldn't help thinking this way. Guess Jax had my mind all messed up.

"Have you prayed?"

Now those were not the first words I expected her to say. "No."

"Well, that's where we need to start." Pastor grabbed my hand and bowed her head. All I could do was follow her. "Heavenly Father, we come to You today with praise and thanksgiving in our hearts for this wonderful gift You have given us—the gift of prayer. Where we can come to You at any time, Lord, and ask for Your forgiveness. Where we know that once we ask for forgiveness, Lord, that it is done. You said in Your Word that as far as the East is from the West that's how much You will forgive us. All we have to do is confess and repent. So, we come to You now because we know that sins confessed are sins forgiven. . . ."

Then Pastor stopped. I kept my eyes and my mouth closed because I knew she couldn't possibly be waiting for *me* to continue. I mean, I'd prayed before, but mostly by myself. There were times in children's church where they made us pray out loud, and I always hated that because I never knew what to say. And even though I was grown up now, it wasn't like I had learned how to talk to God.

But Pastor just stayed quiet. And so did I. Finally she whispered, "Diamond, speak from your heart."

I squeezed my eyes tight and wished there was a way for me to get out of this. But since there wasn't, I just said, "God, I'm so sorry . . . I know I wasn't supposed to have sex, because I'm only fifteen. But I wanted Jax to like me. And even though I had sex with him, he doesn't like me. But I want You to like me. And I don't want You to be mad. So please forgive me. I'm really, really sorry. I've never been so sorry about anything in my whole life. Especially after the way Jax acted. But even if he didn't act that way, I would still be sorry. Because I know what I did was wrong. I wouldn't have wanted to keep doing it. But maybe it is better that Jax didn't talk to me because now You know and I know that I won't have sex with him anymore. I won't do it again. I don't plan to ever have sex again. Ever in life. Amen."

When I looked up, I wanted to die. That had to have been the dumbest prayer Pastor Ford had ever heard, because she was smiling. Almost laughing. I was so embarrassed. I didn't know if God was big on laughing, but if He was, I was sure that right about now, He and everyone in heaven were having a pretty good laugh because of me.

"Pastor, can I try it again?"

"What?"

"The prayer. Can I do it over?"

"Why would you want to do that?"

"Because I didn't get it right and I really am sorry. I want God to know that so that He'll forgive me."

"Diamond, you don't have to do it over. God knew what you were going to say before you even said it. He knows your thoughts, He knows what's on your mind before you even know."

I'd heard Pastor say that before, but I didn't get it. If He knew, then why would He make me go through all of this trouble? "If He knows, then why do we have to pray?"

"That's the way He wants it. He wants us to talk to Him. He wants us to have a relationship with Him, and you can only have a relationship with someone if you talk to them."

"It just seems like if He already knows, we'd be boring Him."

"You don't ever have to worry about that. God loves to hear your voice. Think of it like this, Diamond. There are times when your parents know what you're going to say or do. But just because they know doesn't mean they don't want to talk to you about it. Because through talking, you'll learn something. And they may even learn something. It's the same with God. Talking with Him, you'll hear a few things and learn a few things."

I nodded, although I can't say that I really understood what she was talking about. I'd heard Pastor say so many times that prayer was a dialogue, not a monologue, that we were supposed to do as much listening as talking to God. But God had never said a word to me. Maybe that came when you turned eighteen or something.

"That was a very good prayer," Pastor Ford continued, "because you were honest and sincere. And it all came from your heart. That's all that God wants. But there is one thing . . ."

Oh, no. I knew it. I knew I'd gotten something wrong.

Pastor said, "That part at the end where you said you were never going to have sex again. Your husband might have a different opinion about that."

I shook my head. "After Jax, I don't know if I'll ever get married."

"Diamond, please." The pastor waved her hands as if what I said was ridiculous. "There's no need for you to be so dramatic. Do you think you're the first girl this has happened to?"

Dang, did she have to go there? "No."

"Good. 'Cause you're not. And believe it or not, it's happened to boys. Boys have been tricked into having sex, too. But that's not really the issue. The point I'm making is that we all make mistakes. The key is how we handle our mistakes. How do we bounce back? How do we step up to the new beginnings?"

My head was starting to hurt. This was all a bit complicated to me.

"God's given you a new slate, Diamond. He loves you. Just wants you to get better every day. To get stronger in Him. To be more obedient to Him."

"I want to be good, Pastor. And really, I didn't think I was being all that bad with Jax because I thought I loved him. And we did everything to make sure that I didn't get pregnant or get a disease."

"Is that why you think you shouldn't have had sex? To prevent pregnancy or disease?"

"Yeah," I said, trying not to make it sound like I thought that was a stupid question. "Everyone is always warning us about teenage pregnancies and all the diseases out there. And then, there's also that thing where God says not to do it."

Pastor Ford laughed. "Well, sometimes, just because God said not to, that should be enough. But I know teenagers need more. And *you* definitely need more if you think that abstinence is just to prevent pregnancy and disease. If that's what you think, then I and all the adults around you have failed. Because you've only gotten part of the message.

"We don't want you to get pregnant. And we don't want you to get a sexually transmitted disease. But we talk about abstinence for reasons far beyond those two, Diamond. There're a lot of emotional and psychological consequences and damage that happen because of sex outside of marriage. You're experiencing some of that now because of the way Jax is treating you, right? He's doing and saying things to you that aren't making you feel so good."

I nodded. "And I'm really embarrassed, too."

"Embarrassment and guilt and condemnation . . . that's part of it, too. Sex outside of God's plan is *always* destructive. Always. It never works. And I'm not just saying this because you're a teenager. It doesn't work for adults, either. People who have sex outside of marriage may not see the bad side while they're doing it, but I can guarantee that they always look back with regrets. Even if the regrets come years later. You're always sorry in some way."

"I don't have to wait years to know I'm sorry. I can see all the bad stuff now."

"That's actually a good thing, Diamond. Your lessons have come early."

"That's why I said I don't want to have sex. It just seems safer that way."

"It *is* safer that way. Until you get married. That's when

it's okay with God. That is His wonderful gift to you, and it's a gift that He wants you to cherish."

Just when it was starting to get good, Pastor Ford was making it complicated again. I'd heard this "sex is a gift that should be cherished" before. I didn't get it then—I didn't get it now. It must have been the look on my face that let Pastor Ford know that she was losing me.

"Let me ask you this," Pastor said. "When you were little, did your parents ever give you a gift that you just loved?"

It didn't take me a second to think about that. "Yeah, I got the Millennium Barbie before anyone else!" I said. I still remembered just how happy I was when I woke up on Christmas. I'd asked my parents and every one of my aunts and uncles for that doll. I'd even written a letter to Santa Claus, even though I hadn't believed in him since I was five. I just wanted to make sure, just in case, so that I would get that doll. And on Christmas morning, I did.

"How did you treat that doll?"

"I loved her. I didn't play with her a lot because I didn't want her to get messed up. Everyone said they didn't make many Black Millennium Barbies."

Pastor Ford nodded. "Did you let anyone else play with her?"

"Only Vee, and only a little. I took care of her and I still have it."

"Sounds to me like you cherished that doll. You were careful with her in how you treated her and who you let play with her. You only shared her with Veronique because it was a gift that was special to you."

"Uh-huh."

"Sex is just like that. A special gift from God that He

gives to be used between two people—a man and his wife. It's a gift that God gives to you to give to your husband. And it's a gift that God will give to your husband to give to you. In any other way, you're giving that gift to someone who should not have it. And bad things can happen. People get hurt, get sick, some even die. That's not what God intended with sex."

Pastor had told us this when we took those purity classes before we took the vows to stay virgins. It didn't make a lot of sense to me then, but it did now. Maybe it was because of all that I'd been through.

I just wish that I'd really gotten that special-gift message before. Because I'm sure I wouldn't have given my gift to Jax!

Pastor said, "I wish I'd done a better job of emphasizing this to you before. Maybe it would have helped with the decisions you were faced with when it came to Jason."

See, that's what I was talking about. Pastor Ford just seemed to know what you were thinking. Like God had whispered it in her ear or something.

"But," Pastor continued, "there's nothing we can do about the past. There is, however, lots we can do about the future." She stopped, and whenever Pastor looked at me this way, I got a little scared. She said, "Maybe one day, we can have a session and you can talk to the other girls about what happened to you. Maybe if they hear that, it may help one of them."

"No!" I knew I'd screamed, but I didn't care. There was no way she was going to get me to tell anyone else about this. Already too many people knew. How embarrassing! "If that's my punishment, then I'd rather have something else!"

"Hold on a minute, Diamond. I'm not talking about punishing you. Do you think you should be punished?"

I paused for a moment, wondering if this was a trick question. "Well, I'm still grounded, but I don't want to be punished by having to talk to other girls about this."

"I was just making a suggestion. If you don't want to do it, that's fine."

"Pastor, I don't even want anyone else to know."

"Why?"

"Because it's *embarrassing*. And I'm sorry. I won't do it again. Honest." I sounded as if I was begging. And I was. I wanted to get right on my knees and beg Pastor and God not to tell anyone else.

"You don't have anything to be embarrassed about. And I can tell you that it will really help if you talk to other girls."

I was shaking my head so hard I thought I would get a headache. "I don't want to."

"All right. Maybe not right now. Maybe one day."

Maybe never! That's what I almost told her. But I just kept shaking my head until she got the message.

"Well, there is one thing I do want you to do for me."

Didn't Pastor get it? I wasn't saying anything to anybody about me and Jax. Ever.

She said, "You can go out there with the Divine Divas and win this thing for Hope Chapel."

Whew! I guess Pastor thought she was funny, 'cause she was smiling. I wasn't. I was still shaking at that dumb suggestion she had. Like I would really stand on some stage and have people stare at me while I told them about what a fool I was. Please! That would *never* happen.

"Okay, so are you ready to be part of the group?"

"Yes." I stood up; I couldn't wait to get out of that office.

"Okay, go on. I'm sure the other divas are ready for you. And you're definitely ready to be a diva again."

I only smiled as I hugged Pastor. And I kept my mouth shut even though I wanted to let her know that I wasn't ready to be a diva *again*. I was already one. I always had been and always would be . . . a diva!

I don't know why my heart was beating fast. Maybe it was because I was getting back with my girls. Or maybe it was because I felt as if I'd just made the big escape from Pastor's office. But no matter why . . . I was excited.

The music was blasting and I could hear my girls singing. I had to admit, they sounded fierce, even without me. But it was time for me to join the group again and help my girls rise to a higher level.

I took a deep breath, then busted through the door. "Surprise!"

The track kept playing, but everything else stopped. My crew and Sybil just stood still, staring at me like I was some kind of alien. Their mouths were wide open, but not one word was coming from any of them.

"I guess you're not glad to see me."

"What are you doing here?" Aaliyah asked.

Now in my old life, I would have gotten an attitude. But after everything I'd been through, even Aaliyah's mouth sounded wonderful to me. "Well, if that's the way you're going to welcome me back, I'll just take my behind home." I marched back to the door, but just like I knew, my girls came running after me.

"You'd better get back here!" Aaliyah shouted. Of course, she was the first one to reach me. She grabbed my arm. "Are you back for real?" she asked, and then hugged me.

"Uh-huh!" I knew I probably looked stupid the way I was grinning, but my happy was all the way back when I hugged India and Veronique, too.

"So what happened?" Veronique asked.

I gave them the short version. "My parents said that I could come back."

"So you're not grounded anymore?" India asked.

"I'm still grounded. I can't do the dance team, and I don't have my phone. But it's all good 'cause I'm back with the divas!"

"Yay!" my girls cheered.

"Well, if there are any ladies in the room who want to be divas, they'd better get to working!" Sybil sounded like she was serious, but she was grinning just like the rest of us. She gave me a hug.

"That's right," Turquoise added before she gave me a hug. "I wanna see if y'all can move in these outfits. Let's get back to work."

"That's fine with me," Aaliyah said. " 'Cause I just want to get this over with, because you know I don't really want to be here . . ."

But even though we all knew what she was going to say, we didn't hear her, because Sybil had our track on blast. I jumped in line with India and Aaliyah, and we did the whole routine right behind Veronique.

I might have missed a week, but I didn't miss a beat now. I was fierce, the way I was twisting and turning, swirling and stepping.

We sang. We danced. And then we changed into the outfits that Ms. Tova had designed especially for each of us. Dressed like the divas we were, we practiced for another four hours.

It felt like I had been with my girls all week. Like none of that crazy stuff with Jax had even happened. I was so glad to be back. So glad to be with my girls.

And so glad to be a Divine Diva!

32

I had that heart attack feeling again.

I wasn't worried about singing the words. I could sing our song backward. But these steps? Well, not the steps actually—it was more like steppin' in these boots. These four-inch heels were fierce, but now I wished I'd chosen something more sensible. Like the flat pumps India was wearing. With the silver star on the toe, they were off the chain. But best of all, they were flat. She'd be able to hop and dance all over that stage without any worries.

At least Turquoise had been smart enough to make us practice the last two days in our shoes. I hadn't missed a step in practice, and I hoped to be okay tonight. I would be. I just had to be.

"I have an announcement to make," India said. We all turned to her. "Well, it's not really an announcement. I just have something for you guys." She handed all of us boxes. "But don't open it until I say so." After a few moments, she said, "On the count of three. One, two . . ."

She didn't get to three before I tossed the top off my box. "Oh, my God!" I pulled the silver and black and rhinestone earrings from the box. And so did Veronique and Aaliyah.

"These are gorgeous," Veronique and Aaliyah said at the same time.

"I made them for us. They're all different, but kinda look the same. Like our outfits."

"You made these?" I held the earrings up to my ears. The silver and black crystals matched our dresses, and the rhinestones added just the right amount of bling. I liked these much better than the ones I'd picked out at the mall.

"Hey, look," Aaliyah said. "The hooks have two little Ds."

"For Divine Divas," India said.

"Oh, these are hot," Veronique said right before she slipped her earrings on. "My sistah, you should think about selling these."

That was exactly what I'd been thinking. I didn't know my girl India had this in her. With my flair for fashion and some of her designs, we could build an empire. But first I guess we had to win this contest.

"Okay, ladies, the earrings are nice, but I want you to get back to focusing. Does anyone want any water?"

India grabbed a bottle, but I didn't want anything. Seeing these earrings had calmed me down for a moment, but now my stomach was back to twirling. I couldn't figure this out. I'd wanted to be a star my entire life. I was born to be famous. Born to be standing on a stage in front of thousands of adoring fans.

But for some reason, I was nervous.

Maybe it would have helped if I'd had a chance to peep the competition. Then I would have known for sure that we would be fine. But Sybil had kept us locked away in our dressing room. We'd been back here for forty-five minutes, but it felt like forty-five hours.

"How many groups are there?" I asked Sybil for the millionth time.

But before she could answer me for the millionth time, someone banged on the door.

"Divine Divas!" A lady barged into our room. She said something into the headphones she was wearing before she told us, "You're on in ten."

"Okay, ladies," Sybil clapped, "let's pray."

We grabbed each other's hands; I was surprised to feel that Veronique's hands were sweaty. I guess I wasn't the only one who was nervous. And for the very first time since we started, I was glad that she was the lead and not me.

"We're going to go around and each say a little prayer," Sybil said.

Oh, no. Didn't we already have enough pressure? We had to be on stage in ten minutes. Now on top of all of that, I had to think of something to say to God.

Of course, Aaliyah started, "Lord, we thank you for bringing us here. For letting us get this far. And whatever you have for us now, we'll accept. Thank you."

Then Veronique said, "Lord, I pray for your best for me and my sistahs, because nothing will ever beat your best."

Wow, that was a good word. I didn't know my girl could pray like that.

India prayed, "Father, help us as we go out there. Help us to represent You the way You want us to. Help us to show everyone how much we love You."

Okay, this was ridiculous. Even India knew how to pray. Sybil should've had us practicing praying if she wanted me to do this now.

I wanted to stall, but that wouldn't have done any good. So I just started, "Father, do your thing and we'll do ours.

We want You with us. We need You with us. Thank You."

"Amen!" Sybil said. "Ladies, it's showtime!

It took only minutes for the stage crew to mike us up and run sound checks even though another group was performing. Sybil had us standing behind the curtains so that we couldn't see the act on stage, but I was still trying to grab a peek. Whoever they were, they sounded all right. I'd never heard their song before—a kind of hip-hop version of "Blessed Assurance." Even though Sybil was talking, trying to give us last-minute advice, I kept my ears on that group. Sounded like there were a couple of girls and a couple of guys singing.

Wow, I hadn't thought of that. A mixed group. Guys and girls. Maybe that would have been better. . . .

What? Was I crazy? How could anyone—guys or girls— be better than my crew? We were going to win this thing. All I had to do was believe it.

The sudden cheer from the crowd scared me a little bit. I knew this was the Kodak Theatre, but I wasn't expecting *that* much noise. And I certainly didn't expect anybody to be getting *that* much applause—except for us, of course.

"Let's hear it once again for The Faithful Five," the announcer said.

Then the group—three guys and two girls—came strutting off the stage as if they'd already won. They were all excited, laughing and hugging each other. You would have thought that the contest was over. It took them a minute to see us standing there.

I couldn't believe the way they stared us down—the girls

and the guys—like they were trying to intimidate us or something. Guess no one had told them who we were.

They needed to recognize: We were the Divine Divas. All anyone had to do was look at us and look at them. We were rocking our designer outfits. But they, in their ordinary blue suits and white blouses and navy skirts, looked like missionaries. Hadn't anyone told them that this search was for a young, hip act? I didn't care how much love they got from the audience—the audience obviously hadn't seen us yet.

I put my hand on my hip, twirled on my toes like I was a ballerina, and turned to my girls. "Y'all ready to win this?"

As if we had practiced this moment, my girls followed me, leaving The Faithful Five to stare at our backs.

Now I know this was kind of a Christian competition, and we were supposed to be nice, and humble, and all of that good stuff, but those five whatevers shouldn't have messed with us. 'Cause now I was feelin' like a diva for real.

"Ladies and gentlemen, from Hope Chapel in Inglewood, California, please welcome the Divine Divas."

The way the crowd cheered now, it sounded as if half of the auditorium was filled with members from our church. Too bad we weren't being judged by the applause. We would've won for sure.

We rushed to the stage and took our places, and then the track was cued up. I took one deep breath. And in that moment, I thought about how we'd gotten to this place— how I'd found out about the contest and convinced my girls to do this with me. And now we were here. On the stage. Ready to do our thing.

No matter what happened, I already felt like a winner.

The music started and we began moving, dancing and strutting like we had always been performing forever. Like we were born to do this.

"I don't wanna go to the club," Veronique sang, *"but I want to dance. . . ."*

India, Aaliyah, and I stepped like we'd been doing for nine weeks. But for some reason (maybe it was the stage) we seemed to lift our legs higher and move our hands with more attitude than we'd had in rehearsals.

Then it was our turn to sing. *"I need a DJ who's bumping. . . ."*

We stepped, we turned, we dipped. We performed!

I was so focused on making the right moves that I didn't even think about looking into the crowd—not even when it was my turn to sing my solo. I kept my eyes on the back of the room the way Sybil had told us to do.

We were at the last verse when Veronique shocked us. "Come on, y'all," she yelled to the crowd, "put your hands together!" She clapped her hands above her head, and we did it, too, keeping everything else the same as we'd practiced.

It sounded like a roar when the crowd joined in and started singing with us. For the first time, I took a peek into the audience, but I couldn't see a thing. It was pitch-black out there. Didn't matter though—we couldn't see them. But every single one of them could see us.

"I don't wanna go to the club," the audience sang along. *"But I want to dance."*

Even as we strutted in the single line off the stage the way we'd practiced, the crowd was still singing. And then they started screaming for us.

We were barely off the stage when I yelled, "We did it!"

"Ladies and gentlemen, let's hear it for the Divine Divas."

We ran back onto the stage and bowed again. Sybil had told us that we could only stay out there for a couple of seconds, but I wanted to stay in that place forever. I wanted to do the entire performance again—over and over until I got tired. And I didn't think that I would get tired very soon.

India had to almost pull me off of that stage. Behind the curtains we started doing what that group right before us had been doing—we hugged, and kissed, and jumped around as if *we* had just won the contest. I don't know how it happened, but in seconds we were surrounded by everyone—Pastor Ford, and all of our parents, and even some other people from the church.

"You were just wonderful," my mother said as she wrapped her arms around me. "Who knew you were such a performer."

"Oh, come on, Elizabeth," my father said before he kissed me. "You've got to be kidding. Our little girl was born to be a star."

See, even my daddy knew! It was so good to have him back. In the past few days when he hugged and kissed me, I felt like he really wanted to again. I guess he'd finally forgiven me about that Jax stuff. But, I didn't want to think about any of that right now. All I wanted to do was just stay in this fabulous moment.

"Ah, y'all are going to have to clear this area," the lady with the headphones said. "There are other groups to perform, you know."

Sybil led the way back to our dressing room.

The room sure had changed while we'd been on stage. It was filled with flowers—lots of them. Roses and carnations, and even my favorite—sunflowers. And then there was food—sandwiches and sodas and cookies.

Suddenly, I was starving, but before I could get to the cookies, my mother said, "Divas, we have something for you."

My father and Aaliyah's dad both held two large boxes, and we each grabbed our gifts.

I screamed, knowing I was going to have a heart attack for real when I pulled my bag from the box. It was that Susej designer purse that I had been begging my mother for. But she'd told me that I either had to have a job or win the lottery if I wanted one of these. Now I was holding my own.

"Thank you," I screamed.

And then I turned to my girls—they each had their own bag, too. I was so glad; how great was this?

"Look, that's us," India said.

I looked at my bag more closely. On the front was a hand-painted picture—of us! The Divine Divas. This was too cool.

Pastor Ford said, "Girls, we all want you to know that we are very proud of you. So those bags are a gift from your parents and the members of the church."

"Thank you, Pastor," we all said together.

"It doesn't matter what happens from this point on, you ladies are our stars."

"Weren't they good?" Jackie, the minister of music, added. "We should think about producing a CD through the church."

"Yeah, you ladies would sell a million copies," said Deacon Brown, a man who never smiled. But he was grinning tonight.

I couldn't get enough. My happy was all the way back.

It was like we had all forgotten why we were here. Because about thirty minutes later, when the lady with the headphones banged on our door, we were all shocked.

"Divine Divas, you're wanted on stage."

"Oh, my," my mother said. "Does this mean you won?"

My father hugged me. "God's blessings, sweetheart," he said right before I rushed from the room with Sybil and my crew.

Before we went back to the stage, Sybil said, "Ladies, I just want you to know that you're already winners to me."

The headphone lady pushed us out there, next to a group of three who looked like they were from the movie *Dreamgirls*. Someone needed to check their IDs. They didn't look like teenagers to me. It seemed we were the only ones who got it—they were looking for a young, hip group. And from what I could see, we seemed to be the only ones who could give them that.

India grabbed my hand; I didn't have to look to know that she was also holding onto Veronique and Veronique was holding onto Aaliyah.

The announcer said, "And now, The Faithful Five."

Oh, no. Why did they have to call them, too? And on top of that, put them right next to us? Well, the good thing about it, standing next to The Faithful Five made us look really good.

They tried that staring down thing again, but they were standing next to the wrong one. Aaliyah didn't play with anybody. "Whatcha looking at?" she asked the guy closest to her.

He turned away like he was embarrassed.

See, that was why she was my girl. She might have been

the brains, but she was tough—her daddy's daughter. Nobody messed with Aaliyah.

For the next ten minutes, they kept calling groups to the stage. I wasn't sure if it was everyone who performed, but whatever it was, at least we were there. Finally, when we were packed together, the announcer said, "Ladies and gentlemen, we'd like to bring onto the stage Roberto Hamilton, the president of Glory 2 God Productions."

I leaned forward to see him, and I couldn't believe it—this man could've been P. Diddy's twin. And the way he strutted out, in his oversized shirt and jeans, wearing dark glasses even though we were inside a dark auditorium, he looked like a hip-hop mogul for real.

This was not the kind of man I'd expected to be running a Christian company. But I was glad, 'cause that just gave us a better chance of winning. He had to feel our energy, see our flava. We were the best ones on the stage.

"Thank you for coming out tonight and supporting us," Mr. Hamilton said. "This project has been my dream for a couple of years. I've wanted to bring God back into our music in a real way. Because you see, if you want to reach young people, you've got to meet them where they are. And that's what this contest is all about. So I want to thank you for your support. But most importantly, I want to thank these young people who joined us tonight. Weren't they off the chain?"

The crowd cheered; I'd been feelin' all the applause before, but now I was ready for this to end. All of this wondering and waiting was getting to me.

"So, now, I'd like to announce the two groups who will represent Los Angeles in the state finals."

Finally!

But then I got scared. Ever since I'd found this contest in the magazine, I'd wanted to win, and I'd been sure that we would. But now I wondered if we had done enough. Had we picked the right song? Had we worn the right clothes? Did we stand out?

I bowed my head and prayed inside. *Father, I haven't been the best one of your children. But I want to be. And I really want to win this contest. Please, God. Please.*

I squeezed India's hand, and she squeezed back.

Roberto said, "The first group going to San Francisco is . . . The Faithful Five."

Oh, God. For a moment, I thought I was going to faint right there. Of all the people to win, why did it have to be the missionaries? Everyone around us was clapping, so I clapped, too. But at the same time, I kept talking to God.

Okay, Lord. He said there were two groups. So, let's try this again. I hope that you heard me. Please, please, please. . . .

"And the other group representing Los Angeles is . . . the Divine Divas!"

The auditorium exploded in cheers again, and I was almost sure that I heard my mother screaming.

"We won, Diamond. We won!"

My girls were hugging me. And crying. Even Aaliyah was jumping up and down like she really wanted to be there.

We stepped to the front of the stage, holding hands like the sisters we were.

"Ladies and gentlemen, give it up for these young people and all of the groups tonight. Now, we hope to see you in San Francisco. Come out and support your L.A. winners. See you in February. Good night and God bless!"

As soon as Mr. Hamilton said good-bye, the other

groups on the stage surrounded us with lots of love and congratulations. I was impressed, 'cause I didn't know if I would have been as nice if we hadn't won. I probably would have walked right off that stage. I guess I got a few lessons on how to handle this in a Christian way.

Finally, Sybil pulled us off, and when we got backstage, we bumped into The Faithful Five.

"I guess we'll see you in San Francisco," one of the girls said.

Before I could throw my attitude to her, India stepped up. "Yeah, we'll be there. And we'll be ready. The question is, will you be?" And then India whipped around as if she always put people in their place.

Whoa. I guess winning gave all of us a bit of confidence. I wanted to give my girl a high five, but I could tell by the look on Sybil's face that she wasn't really feelin' our attitudes. I knew a "Christian lecture" would be coming soon. Probably at the next practice.

But for now, I was really proud of India. The Faithful Five had started it; we had to stand up for ourselves and show them that we would throw down if it came to that. We weren't walking away from anyone.

But I didn't want to take up my brain space thinking about The Faithful Five right now. All I wanted to do was to stay here and remember this time. The time when we went out there to that big ole stage and did our thing. The time when, for just a little while, I got a chance to forget the problems I'd had over the last couple of weeks.

When I thought about Jax, I felt like such a loser. But with the Divine Divas, I was a winner for sure. And not just for tonight. I had a feeling that no matter what happened, we were going to be winners for a long, long time.

33

I was a winner.

I had to keep telling myself that, even though everyone around me was telling me the same thing. The entire Thanksgiving weekend, every friend and relative we saw told me how proud they were of me and my girls.

But for some reason, I couldn't get my happy all the way back. It was this thing with Jax. I couldn't get it—or him—out of my mind. After winning the contest, I'd go to sleep thinking about the Divine Divas, but then I'd dream about Jax. And I'd feel bad all over again about just how dumb I'd been. I guess these were some of the consequences that Pastor had talked about—these bad feelings that stayed inside you for a long time.

I had thought that staying away from Jax would have helped me. After he'd told me all that stupid stuff, I'd only seen him once or twice in school. And it had always been from far away—which had been a good thing.

The only time I'd been afraid of seeing Jax had been in the cafeteria. And I'd stayed away from there, telling my girls that I'd still been working on extra credit to make up my grades. But extra credit nothing; every day I'd eaten my lunch somewhere different—in the bathroom, or on the back of the school stairs, or in an empty classroom.

But over the Thanksgiving weekend, I decided this was ridiculous. Why was I running away from Jax? He didn't own the school, and he'd been just as wrong as I'd been. I was tired of feeling sorry for myself, tired of feeling bad. I was a winner, and I was going to start acting like it.

On our first day back after Thanksgiving—and winning the contest—I held my head up, tossed my new designer purse over my shoulder, and marched right into the cafeteria for lunch.

"Well, what blew you in here today?" Veronique asked. "You're going to eat with us?"

"Yeah."

"Guess 'cause you're a star now, you can join us," India laughed.

"First of all, I've always been a star," I said. "Second of all, y'all are stars, too. And third of all, I finished doing all of my extra work, so I can come back to lunch."

"Good thing," Aaliyah said. "I thought you were trying to take my place. Doing all of that extra credit, everybody would have said that you were the great student and not me." She grinned.

"Is that how you really want to be known?"

Aaliyah nodded. "What's wrong with that?"

"I'd think you'd want to be known as one of the Divine Divas."

"That too, I guess." She tried not to smile.

I was so glad she'd come around. I wouldn't have been the star I was without her or India and Veronique.

"Attention, Holy Cross Prep. Attention." The scratchy voice came over the loudspeaker. It wasn't often that the principal made an announcement. So the cafeteria got pretty quiet.

"This is a special message. We'd like to congratulate Holy Cross Prep's very own Divine Divas: Diamond Winters, India Morrow, Veronique Garrett, and Aaliyah Reid."

I was shocked. And the way my girls looked—all stiff and surprised—showed me they were shocked, too. Even India had put her fork down.

"These ladies won the city championships for the Glory 2 God Gospel Talent Search and are on their way to San Francisco to compete in the state finals. Let's all congratulate these ladies—Holy Cross's very own divas!"

The students cheered, and some of them began floating over to our table, congratulating us. Even some of the basketball players came over.

I was feeling good. Until Jax walked by. With Jayde.

The two of them strolled past our table, arm in arm. Didn't pay a bit of attention to us, like they hadn't heard the announcement—or if they'd heard it, like they didn't care.

There were plenty of guys sitting at our table now, wanting to hear all about the Divine Divas. But I couldn't help watching Jayde and Jax. It was clear they were really a couple. The way he helped her with her tray. And then the way he kissed her before he paid for her lunch. Then they sat at one of the smaller tables.

When a couple of his boys tried to join him, Jax waved them away, as if he didn't want to be bothered with anyone or anything besides Jayde.

I wondered what it was that made Jax like Jayde so much?

It must've been the way I was staring that made Aaliyah say, "I can't stand that boy."

It was beginning to sound like the words to a bad song—she said that every time she saw Jax.

"I'm so glad you finally gave up on him," she added.

Veronique looked over to where Jax was sitting with Jayde, but when she looked back at me, she didn't say a word.

I said, "Yeah, I'm glad I gave up on him, too. Jax wasn't really my type anyway."

Aaliyah said, "Well, I'm glad, because word is that he and Jayde keep breaking up because he's such a dog."

I glanced at Jax once again. Stared at the back of his head for a moment and wished that things had been different with us. Wished that he had really liked me. The way he seemed to like Jayde.

I asked her, "What do you mean he's a dog?" He didn't seem like much of a dog to me right now. Not the way he was holding Jayde's hand.

Aaliyah lowered her voice. "Well, what I heard was that Jax keeps trying to get Jayde to sleep with him, but she won't. That's why they keep breaking up."

It was a good thing that none of my girls could see what was going on inside of me, because the way my heart was beating would have given it all away. I just hoped that I didn't have a heart attack for real!

Aaliyah kept going, "But the thing that is so funny is Jax keeps going back to Jayde. He just can't seem to get enough of her. I guess not having sex with him is working."

There wasn't a bigger dummy on earth than me. Now I really wished that things could have been different. I wished that I had never met Jason Xavier.

The way Veronique looked at me, I wondered if she somehow knew. But then I thought, no way, because none of my girls ever held back what they were thinking. But I couldn't help but remember what Veronique had told me— the only way to keep the boy is to keep the boy waiting.

Looked like my girl had been right. And somehow, Jayde Monroe had gotten that message. Seemed like I was the only one who hadn't believed that—until now.

Pastor Ford said that I had made a mistake but that I could start all over. Well, that was exactly what I was going to do.

I looked over at Jax and Jayde once again. Whatever, whatever.

"I don't care anything about Jax and Jayde," I said. And for the first time I meant it. "And do you know why?"

"Why?" my crew all asked at the same time.

" 'Cause I'm a star. And 'bout to be a bigger one. San Fran and everyone in that city better watch out." I meant every word, too. I'd read in a magazine that success was the best revenge, and I was about to have a whole lotta success.

Suddenly I pushed my lunch to the side and jumped on top of the table. "I'm a Divine Diva," I yelled.

I cracked up when Veronique jumped on the table with me. And then India and Aaliyah did, too. We had to hold hands to balance ourselves, but that was no problem. Because that was just what we did. Held onto each other and held each other up.

"We're the Divine Divas," I yelled again. And then we held our hands up high.

The cafeteria exploded. "Divine Divas, Divine Divas, Divine Divas," they cheered.

We were winners for sure.

Reader's Group Guide

Summary

When Diamond hears that Glory 2 God Productions is looking for a hot new youth gospel act to sign, she rallies her best friends India, Veronique, and Aaliyah, and they quickly form the Divine Divas. While preparing for the regional competition Diamond must also juggle her new role as sophomore on the varsity dance team and keep her grades up. This all gets a lot harder when she starts talking to and flirting with Jax, the senior star of the basketball team. When Jax asks Diamond out she is thrilled, but her girlfriends are wary of Jax's reputation. Soon all Diamond can think about is Jax and their budding relationship. Before long she is lying to her parents, her friends, and maybe even herself. When Jax suggests they have sex to secure their tenuous bond, Diamond finds herself wondering if this is just the thing to keep them together.

1. Diamond says that she "loved [her] crew like they were [her] own sisters" (page 2). In what ways do the Divine Divas treat each other as family? Do you have any friends you think of as family? What is the difference between "sisters" and "sistahs" as you see it?

2. Do you think all of the girls are motivated to form the Divine Divas for the same reasons? Which girls seem driven by the money and fame? Does anyone seem to be in it for the friendship? Or to offer praise to God through singing?

3. Diamond seems to get all of her advice on love and fashion from magazines. To whom do you go when you need some advice? Do you talk to your friends, parents, teachers, or neighbors? Do you think magazines are a good source for dating advice?

4. Discuss Diamond's relationships with her parents. How does she view her mother as being different from her father? Do you think their rules for her are fair? Did any of their actions end up surprising you?

5. When Diamond begins talking to Jax, her friends don't seem to approve. What do they see in Jax that Diamond is blind to? What did you, as a reader, notice about Jax that might be a warning sign for how he would eventually treat Diamond?

6. Were you surprised about how Diamond's parents and Pastor Ford reacted to Diamond's news about her night with Jax? Do you think that they were successful in helping

Diamond recognize where she went wrong, and how to make better decisions in the future?

7. Do you think Diamond's experiences with a player like Jax are common for sophomores in high school? Were the characters in the book believable as high school students?

8. Veronique tells Diamond that "the only way to keep the boy is to keep the boy waiting" (page 229). Do you think this is true in Jax's case? Do you think that is always the proper approach?

9. Throughout the book Diamond talks about her "happy" as a noun. She views her contentment as tangible, something she can see and touch, and something that someone else can take away. Who and what affects her "happy"? How can she take more control of keeping her "happy" in place?

10. Pastor Ford asks Diamond if she would ever be willing to speak to other girls at the church about what happened between her and Jax. Why do you think Diamond refuses so quickly? Do you think she has reason to be embarrassed? Do you think she has an opportunity to help other teens by sharing her story?

11. Discuss Diamond's relationship with God. Do you think her religious views changed at all over the course of the novel?

12. At the City Championships there is some tension between the Divine Divas and the Faithful Five. How did the

girls handle themselves? Do you think they showed maturity? What would you have done?

13. What lessons did you as a reader take away from the story? What did you learn about love from Diamond's experiences with Jax? What did you learn about friendship from the relationships among the Divine Divas?

14. Diamond's story is the first in The Divas series. Whose story do you most look forward to reading? With which girl do you most identify? What do you think the future holds for the Divine Divas? Are they prepared for a life of fame?

Enhancing Your Book Club

1. Make a mix CD of songs by youth gospel choirs, like the Divine Divas, to play at your book club meeting.

2. Diamond, India, Veronique, and Aaliyah have fun trying to come up with a name for their singing group. Come up with a name for your book club. Try putting your names together, or working in the name of your neighborhood, church, or school.

3. India makes personalized Divine Diva earrings for the performance. If you are hosting the book club, collect some materials so that members can make personalized bookmarks.

4. Visit the author's website at www.victoriachristopher murray.com. You can also visit her at www.thedivine divas.com to see what else she is working on. You can even sign her guest book with your book club's new name and let her know what you thought of *Diamond*.

5. Are some of the lessons you learned from Diamond's story reflected in the Bible? Can you pick out any verses you'd like to share with the book club?

A Conversation with
Victoria Christopher Murray

Q. You've written a number of novels for adults during your career. What compelled you to write for a younger audience?

A. On many of my tours, I had the opportunity to speak at high schools. One of the things I noticed and was challenged by was the type of sex-filled books that young girls were reading. I complained about it for a few years and finally realized that as a writer, I could do something about it.

Q. You have said, "I think being a Christian is not an adjective, it's a verb. So in my walk with Christ, I pray that you can see Him in everything I do." Where do you hope readers will see your spirituality coming through in *Diamond*? How did you aim to give glory to God through this work?

A. Hmmm, that's a good question. I guess what I want to show teenagers is that we understand their challenges and their issues. But that no matter what problems they have or mistakes they make, God still loves them, He's still in charge, and He has this great "do over" system (forgiveness) in place. I also hope that this series shows that teenagers (and adults) can be hip and holy—it doesn't have to be one or the other.

Q. Pastor Ford asks Diamond if she would be willing to share the story of her experiences with Jax with other girls in the community. In a way, you've done just that by writing her story. What do you hope your young female readers will learn from Diamond's mistakes? How do you hope this book might affect parent-child relationships among your readership?

A. I want young girls to understand that the pressure they feel to have sex is not a new issue—that issue is as old as time. But I want girls to feel better about opening up to adults—their mothers, an aunt, a godmother—someone. And honestly, I hope mothers and mother figures will read this novel and learn more about how to communicate with teenagers! It has to be a two-way street—if we want to help our daughters in making better decisions, we have to be there to listen with understanding ears, to speak with caring lips, and to love with a forgiving heart.

Q. Did you find it difficult to write about teen issues as an adult? Did you have to adapt your writing process at all? Do you have any trusted young women in your life who helped you remember what it is like to be in high school?

A. First of all, who said I was an adult? Just kidding! (I think.) Anyway, I didn't have to adapt my writing process, just my style. I wrote my teen novels in first person, and I felt as if I was a teenager all over again. There were quite a few young ladies in my life, but what I did most was watch the television shows and listen to the music that teen girls love. Then just like that, I was talking about "fierce," and "peep this," and "rollin' with a sistah."

Q. Do you see yourself in any of the Divine Divas? With which girl do you most identify?
A. None of the girls are patterned after me—they are way cooler than I ever was in high school! But if I had to answer this question, I would say that I'm most like Aaliyah, the studious one. But the truth would be that my heart (and the rest of me) is probably most like Diamond's.

Q. Diamond's story takes place in California, but you grew up on the East Coast. In what ways do you think a young woman's surroundings might affect the issues she deals with on a regular basis? In what ways does Diamond's story resonate with readers of any background?
A. I don't think surroundings (cities or states) affect the issues—I think teenage issues are pretty universal. Whether you live in New York or Nevada, Hollywood or Hawaii, I think the challenges are the same.

Q. From where do you draw your inspiration? Are there other writers whose work influences your own?
A. I find the inspiration question so interesting because I think what inspires many artists is the same thing that inspires everyone. While I absolutely love what I do, it is still my job. I am inspired by wanting to be paid and that doesn't happen unless I write a book. That said, I never run out of ideas or struggle with an idea for my next novel. I am filled with stories. I guess that means that I am internally inspired totally by God.

Q. Diamond learns a valuable lesson about love and sex. How can readers apply the lessons Diamond has learned to other troubles they face in their lives?

A. I think the lesson I want readers to take away is never to lie to themselves. There are enough people out there lying to you—you have to stay true to yourself. I also want young people to find an adult they can trust—someone they can talk to about anything without fear. And then go to that person when issues arise.

Q. Diamond relies so heavily on her Sidekick. Talking with Jax on her phone and texting with him led her to trouble. Do you think that unrestricted access to these technologies can lead teens astray? How can parents help control what their children are doing with their communication devices?

A. I am not a parenting expert, just like I'm not a minister, so I don't feel comfortable giving this kind of advice. But I will say that access to technology has changed the world. When I was a teenager, if anyone wanted to get to me, they had to go through the family phone—and that meant that my mother and father knew who I was talking to. Now communication is direct. And that makes it more dangerous. I don't have answers for what parents can do—that is something that has to be answered by each individual family.

Q. You plan to continue The Divas series, telling each girl's story in a new book. Why did you choose to tell Diamond's story first? What can we expect in the coming books?

A. Okay, this is going to sound like a dumb answer, but I told Diamond's story first because she is the *D* in Diva. Her name, her story comes first! I don't want to give away the other issues with the girls. Let's just say that each girl has to deal with issues that are common to teenagers today.

If you enjoyed *The Divas: Diamond,* don't miss

The Divas: India

Coming soon from Pocket Books

Turn the page for a sneak preview . . .

Hey, is Drama Mama home?" Diamond bounced on my bed so hard the canopy shook.

"Would you stop calling my mom that?" I said like I was mad. But I wasn't. Sometimes I even laughed when Diamond called my mom that.

Anyway, today I wasn't mad at anybody. This was one of the first times since we performed in the assembly last week that I really felt great. All of my BFFs had come home with me to check out the new jewelry designs I'd made for us to wear for the second round of the contest in San Francisco.

"Drama Mama is not so bad," Veronique said to me as she sat at my computer. She turned it on and started playing with the keys. "It's way better than what she calls my mother."

We all had to laugh at that. Diamond called Veronique's mother the Queen . . . of Mean! But just like me, Veronique didn't really seem to care. Sometimes I wondered if it was because she knew that was a good name for her mom. Ms. Lena really was mean, and sometimes she even scared me. But I guess she had to live like that—kind of strict because she had to take care of Veronique and her four brothers. I may have been only fifteen, but I knew I'd be way mad and way mean, too, if I had to take care of five children all by myself.

Aaliyah's backpack made such a thump on the floor, it scared me.

"What do you have in there?" Veronique asked.

"What do you think?" Diamond said. "Nothing but books. Books, books, books. That's all she cares about." Diamond put her hands on her hips. "Don't you ever get tired of studying?"

Aaliyah shrugged. "Don't you ever get tired of never seeing an A?"

I tried not to laugh, but my giggles came out anyway. I couldn't believe Aaliyah went there. But I guess Diamond had it coming. She always gave Aaliyah such a hard time about being a good student. I think in a way, she was kind of jealous. Not that I blamed Diamond. I mean, who wouldn't be a little jealous of all the As Aaliyah got.

"Whatever, whatever." Diamond flicked her fingers across her shoulder like she was brushing off Aaliyah's words. "Anyway, I didn't come over here for all of that." She rubbed her hands together and grinned at me. "Okay, India. We're waiting."

From the moment I told my best friends at lunch about my designs, I'd been excited. Now I wasn't so sure. Suppose they didn't like these new pieces? Suppose they thought that everything I'd made was stupid?

Slowly, I took the black velvet box from my nightstand. But before I could even get it all the way out, Diamond grabbed the box from me. She flipped open the top as Veronique and Aaliyah sat next to her on my bed.

I held my breath as my best friends stared at the silver chains and charms I'd made. A little while ago, I thought my designs were really cool. But the way my BFFs just sat there with their mouths open, I wished I had kept it all to myself.

"These are gorgeous." Aaliyah lifted one of the chains and then jumped up and stood in front of my mirror. Before I knew it, Diamond and Veronique were right behind her doing the same thing with chains they'd pulled from the box.

They were oohing and aahing and giggling so much that finally I remembered to breathe.

"This is the one I want!" Diamond posed in the mirror wearing the triple-strand silver chain that came all the way down to her knees. "This is fierce!"

"Yeah, my sistah." Veronique grinned at me. "I didn't know you had this in you."

"I've got to find something awesome to wear with this." Diamond strutted across my room as if she were a model. "I'm not waiting for San Fran. I'm gonna wear this now. We need to go shopping."

Okay, now see—just when I was starting to feel good, Diamond had to bring up shopping. That's all she ever talked about. I swear, if she had her way, there would be a mall attached to the back of her house.

I hated shopping, especially with my BFFs. I could never wear the same clothes or even shop in the same stores that they did. So whenever we went to the mall, I just walked around with them, carrying their bags and feeling bad.

"Yeah, let's go shopping," Veronique added, making me feel way, way worse. I knew she liked to shop, but Veronique never had any money. And then she said, "I can actually buy something when we hit the mall. My mom said that all the money from my job that I'm making, I can keep for the Divine Divas."

"That's great!" The way Diamond cheered, you would have thought Veronique had just won the lottery or something. "Just make sure that you save some of that money for San Fran. We're gonna have a couple of days there, and we'll really be able to hang in the stores."

"New York is where I really want to go," Veronique said.

"Of course, the N.Y.C. is like triple A when it comes to finding fashion or anything else," Diamond said as if she were some kind of professor of shopping. "But no worries. Being the fashionista that I am, I know some great places in San Fran, too."

"Yeah, I was there with my dad last year," Aaliyah said. "Union Square is the place to go."

Okay, this was bad. Shopping was definitely Diamond's thing and sometimes Veronique's. But I could always count on Aaliyah to hate shopping as much as I did. I guess being a Divine Diva had changed her, too.

I asked, "Why can't we just have my mom's friend make our clothes like we did last time?" thinking that way we could stay away from the mall.

"Now, you know working with Drama Mama's designers was hot, but that's all the more reason why we need to get to the mall. To scope out some outfits. We *need* to shop to get inspired."

Inspired? What kind of inspiration did we need? "Tova's designers can make us anything we want."

Diamond laughed. "You always crack me up, calling your mom Tova. Shoot," she bounced back on the bed, "if I ever called the judge Elizabeth, my mother would slap me so hard I wouldn't even need a plane to get to San Fran."

"You know?" Veronique added. We all knew her mother would do the same thing.

I shrugged. Yeah, I called my mother by her first name. That's how she wanted it—from the time I was a little girl.

I think it made her feel like she was more my friend than my mother. Sometimes it was cool. But most of the time I just wished that she'd let me call her Mom.

"Let's hit the mall this weekend," Diamond said, getting right back to her favorite topic. "This will be my first weekend off punishment, and I need to get started on my Christmas shopping anyway."

"I'm down," Veronique said. "If I don't have to babysit."

Diamond picked up another one of my chains and wrapped the long one around her waist. "I'm thinking, we need to take this fashion stuff seriously. I mean, we're gonna be huge stars, and maybe soon we'll have our own line of clothes. The Divine Divas line."

"Sounds good, my sistah." Veronique laughed.

"Yeah, Diamond. That's the first good idea you've had," Aaliyah said. "You guys can design the clothes and I'll be the CEO and run everything."

Diamond pinched her lips together and made a face. "You'll be the CEO? I thought you were going to be a nuclear physicist or something."

"I can be both."

While my friends debated about their company that didn't even exist, I sat on the floor, crossed my legs yoga-style, and leaned against the wall. Diamond, Veronique, and Aaliyah didn't even notice that I wasn't primping and posing with them.

Now I was almost sorry that I asked them to come over. We were in my house, in my bedroom, and I still felt invisible. It was always like this once the talk turned to clothes and shopping and all the stuff that didn't have a thing to do with me.

Not that I really hated clothes. If I could look as cute as

my friends in anything, I'd always want to go shopping, too. Everything looked good in a size five, seven, or nine. But get that same skirt for a big girl, and you had an elephant wearing a tutu.

"Okay, so we're set for this weekend, right?" Diamond asked.

"I have to work Saturday morning, but as long as I don't have to babysit, I'll be free by noon."

"I'm cool, too," Aaliyah said, "but I don't want to be out all day."

"I know, I know," Diamond said, waving Aaliyah's words away before she got to say anything about wanting to study. Then she glanced around my bedroom like she was looking for something. "India, why're you sitting over there? Come here." She held up the first chain she'd tried on. "I have just two questions. Can I have this one for Christmas?" She laughed, but I knew she was serious. "And my second question is, which one are you gonna wear 'cause we gotta look fierce in San Fran."

I put on a happy face before I pushed up from my hiding place. I already knew which chain I wanted to wear. What I hadn't figured out was what I was going to wear with my chain. I had made up my mind—I wasn't going to San Francisco as a fat girl.

I hooked the chain that I wanted to wear around my neck.

"San Fran here we come," Diamond said and then we all struck a pose in the mirror like we were on the stage. "But first, we gotta go to the mall!"

This time, I laughed with my BFFs. Now all I had to figure out was a way to keep laughing on the outside, and maybe that would help me to stop crying on the inside.

Christian Novels for Teens!